Finding Riley

A Forever Home Novel
Book 2

Dan Walsh

Praise for Some of
Dan Walsh's Other Novels:

Praise for *Rescuing Finley* (Book 1 of this series):

"Anyone familiar with Walsh's books knows he writes great stories with memorable characters, and Rescuing Finley is no exception...I've read several books recently that feature a dog as a main character, but this one is the most realistic I have come across...This book is heart-tugging, thought-provoking and meaningful." — **RT Book Reviews Magazine**

"While you shouldn't always judge a book by its cover, I can vouch for the fact that the story is as heartwarming as the outside of this novel...Walsh is an expert at crafting stories that warm your heart and touch your soul without being syrupy and overly sentimental. I look forward to the next two Forever Home novels." — **Mocha with Linda Blog**

1

Okay, he got it. It was December. But it was also Florida. So why was John Finch still shivering inside his sleeping bag, his body all curled up in a ball?

He'd packed up his things three weeks ago and hitched a freight train down from Memphis to avoid freezing weather like this. Riding a freight train was a scary thing, but John couldn't get the money together for a Greyhound ticket. At the time, it seemed worth the risk. But now?

He heard the tent zipper go down.

"You ever coming outta there, John? Fire's burning nice and hot now. Coffee's all brewed." It was his friend, Alfred. Alfred's the one who'd invited him to this camp. Some of Alfred's friends had nicknamed him Two-Sheets because, most of the time, Alfred stayed slightly inebriated. Not fall down drunk, mind you. Otherwise, they'd have called them Three-Sheets ("three sheets to the wind").

John peeked his head out of the sleeping bag. "What time is it?"

"Almost nine. Starting to see the sun through the trees. Supposed to be the last day of this cold snap. Said so on the radio not twenty minutes ago. So, c'mon. We need to get to work sprucing up the camp for that cameraman who's coming. Don't want him to think the homeless are nothing but lazy bums."

That's right. John couldn't believe it. Some idiot had gone and said yes to a guy making a documentary about the homeless. He'd found out about it last night. "When's this guy supposed to show up?"

"I don't know. What's a-matter? Didn't you sleep okay last night? I certainly did. I always sleep better when it's cold."

John sighed. He might as well just get up. Alfred wasn't gonna stop nagging until he did. And he definitely didn't want to still be in bed when that camera guy started filming their campsite. "All right," he said. "Gimmie a minute. I'll be right out."

"Want me to pour your coffee?"

"That would be nice."

Alfred zipped the tent flap back up "Save you a spot by the fire."

John sat up on his cot, started getting out of his sleeping bag. That was something to be grateful for anyway, not having to sleep on the ground. He'd slept on one of those aluminum camping cots you pick up at Walmart for thirty-five bucks. John didn't pay that, of course. Alfred had snatched it for him the day before John arrived. Some guy was breaking camp and heading south, said he needed to travel light and couldn't take it with him.

Reaching over, John lifted his leather jacket from a crate beside the cot and put it on. He looked down at his boots. They were a little small. He couldn't lace them up wearing anything more than one pair of socks. Right now he had on three. But at least he could feel his toes. How long would that last after shedding two pairs and cramming his feet into those old boots?

He sighed again. Didn't matter. Had to be done.

He did it quickly and stood up just as fast. It was a dome-style tent with decent head room. Alfred bought it used a few months ago. Told John how much he'd paid for it. John figured that was a hint, so he'd given him some money when he got here. Almost half, which is why he didn't have any money for the bus ticket. But now John was having doubts about his investment.

Last night made it three nights in a row where the outside temperature had dipped below freezing. Maybe he could talk Alfred into the two of them taking off in a few days, make their way south.

John knew you got down around Tampa and, while it could still get chilly at night, it was nowhere near this cold. He wasn't exactly sure where they were now. In the woods somewhere a few miles north of a little town called Summerville (at the moment, the name hardly fit). The nearest named-town he recognized was Ocala, maybe a half-hour away.

As he unzipped the tent and stepped outside, he heard Christmas music on a radio somewhere in the distance. Johnny Mathis singing, *It's Beginning to Look a Lot Like Christmas*. No mistaking that distinctive vibrato. Looking around at the sight before him, John couldn't quite agree with Mr. Mathis. It was cold enough to *feel* like Christmas, but it looked just like what it was—a dirty old camp of homeless people living in the woods.

He'd seen plenty of similar camps in several different states over the last two decades, since he'd joined their ranks. This was better than some. Definitely more organized. Alfred had said the two guys who'd been here the longest set things up almost four years ago. Most of the camps John lived in had either fallen apart, or everyone got chased out within a few months.

John walked down the narrow path toward the fire pit, saw a smiling Alfred waving, pointing at an empty canvas chair beside him. A steaming cup of coffee sat on a makeshift table. Though the woods were pretty thick out by the road and for the first hundred yards or so, they opened into a nice clearing where the tents had been set up. Here, only a few shady trees stuck out of the ground every so often, palm trees had sprouted here and there, and lots of skinny saplings were scattered all about.

"There you are," Alfred said. "Nice and toasty over here."

John could feel the heat even this far from the fire. More than the heat, he was aware of that coffee cup. As he walked around and behind Alfred to avoid the smoke, another guy who'd been sitting a few feet away got up and headed toward a tarped area, where breakfast was being served.

"If you're hungry," Alfred said, "maybe you should follow

him. They're not gonna serve breakfast much longer."

John sat and picked up the cup of coffee. "This is all I need. Thanks for getting it."

"No problem."

John took a few slow sips. He stretched out his legs to warm up his boots. Between the fire, the coffee going down smooth, the breakfast smells hanging in the air, and the sun shining through the trees…this wasn't so bad after all. But you could have all this a few hours south and be totally rid of the cold as well. He leaned over in Alfred's direction. "While it's just the two of us here, I want to bring up something we've talked about before."

"I know what you're gonna say already."

"You do? Okay, what is it?"

Alfred stared into the fire. "You're gonna say, we're in Florida. Florida's a long state. What are we doing so far north? Why don't we head further south a few hours? Find a place where we don't freeze our butts off at night." He looked at John. "Am I right?"

"Okay. So maybe I've been talking about this a little too much. But can you blame me? I don't know how you're putting up with this weather. Doesn't it bother your arthritis?"

"It bothers me some. But I'm telling you, John. I ain't ever been in a place like this, where I feel mostly safe at night. You never been attacked before."

"I have, too."

"Not like I have."

He'd almost forgotten. Two years ago, Alfred had been

ambushed in the middle of the night by two guys who'd broken into their camp. Beat him up real good. Stole all his stuff. Took him four days in the hospital to recover. "Okay, not like you have."

Alfred pointed to the guy who'd just left. "See him? He just came up here a few days ago from a camp just south of Orlando. Said a guy in the group he was staying with got hacked to death by some lunatic with a machete. Not beat up, killed. Right in his tent. Happened three nights ago. That's why he left and came up here. I knew you were going to want to talk about this again, so I asked him how cold it was down there, you know, at nighttime. Know what he said? It wasn't bad at all. At night or during the day. I didn't even have to ask him, why then didn't he just stay put. You know why?"

"Okay," John said. "I get it. They ever catch the guys that did it?"

"Nope."

"So they're still out there somewhere."

"Down *there* somewhere," Alfred said. "Not up here."

"You don't know that. If they didn't get caught, what's keeping 'em from making their way up here?"

"They wouldn't do that. No one in their right minds would head north in December, not with it being this cold."

John just stared at him. Did Alfred even realize he'd just admitted they weren't in their right minds either, staying up here where it was so cold? "Never mind," John said.

"Anyway," Alfred said, "that killer could never get into this camp. Too many people. And everyone here knows everyone

6

else. They'd stick out like a sore thumb. Besides that, they don't let just anyone plop a tent down here. It's invite-only. You should-a heard all the questions they asked me before they said yes about you coming in."

John sighed. How did Alfred think any of that made them any more secure than people in homeless camps anywhere else in the state? At night, camps were all the same. Dark. Anyone who wanted to could sneak around in the dark any time they pleased. They could come up here and attack you in the cold, or stay down south and do it where it was nice and warm. "Alright, you win. I won't bring it up again."

Just then, some excitement started up over at the tarped breakfast area. A bunch of people were gathering around. "What's that about?" John said.

"I'm not sure," Alfred said. "Looks like the camera guy. The one making that documentary? I think he just showed up."

"Great," John said. "That's just great."

2

Savannah, Georgia

Now this was kind of exciting. He wasn't sure why just yet, but Riley could tell by the look on everyone's faces, this thing they were doing was a good thing. It made them happy. He liked it when his people were happy.

His tail still wagging, Riley followed close behind the woman. Her name was Mom. She stepped out of the big walk-in closet in the master bedroom and handed a box to Jeffrey. It was too high off the ground for Riley to see inside. But Jeffrey could see it, and his eyes lit up.

"Snowmen," Jeffrey said. "Can I bring these downstairs?"

"That's why I'm giving them to you," Mom said. "But don't take them out of the box yet. Wait till we get all the boxes down. Just stack them on top of the coffee table."

"Okay." He turned toward the stairwell.

"And be careful going down the stairs. That's why I gave you a small box, so you could keep one hand on the rail."

"I will."

His big sister, Lisa, stepped into the same spot and held out her hands. "You can give me a bigger box than that."

Riley started following Jeffrey down the stairs. He always followed Jeffrey, if there was more than one family member in the room. Jeffrey wasn't his leader. Not exactly. But he was the one who'd spent the most time with Riley, the one who treated him the best. Mom was definitely in charge. The man who was mostly called Dad (but sometimes Tom) was also pretty important. But Dad was usually gone most of the day. Like right now.

After going down three steps, Riley had to pass Jeffrey or risk running into the back of his legs. He hurried to the bottom and spun around to greet him. His tail thumped on the oval throw rug. What was in that box and why did it make Jeffrey so happy? He sniffed the air but couldn't pick up any unusual scents.

As Jeffrey carried the box to the coffee table, Riley couldn't help himself. He had to see what was inside. He stood on his hind legs, put his front paws across Jeffrey's arm and licked his ear.

Jeffrey laughed. "Get down, Riley." He lowered his arm. Riley's front legs slid back to the floor. "You sit, and I'll show you what it is."

Riley understood two words: *down* and *sit*. He obeyed.

As he did, footsteps came down the stairs. He turned to see Lisa carrying another box.

"Here," Jeffrey said, holding a white stuffed toy in front of

Riley's face. "It's a snowman. See?" He set it on the coffee table.

Of course, Riley grabbed it in his mouth. He instantly liked the way it felt as he crunched down on it.

"Riley! Drop it!" Lisa yelled, from the bottom of the stairs. He did and instantly lowered his head.

"Don't put that right in front of his face," she said to Jeffrey. "Are you stupid? He'll think it's a toy, just like his squirrel." She set her box on the other end of the coffee table.

"He wasn't going to hurt it," Jeffrey said. "You don't have to yell." He patted Riley on the head. "It's okay, boy. You didn't know, did you?"

"He didn't hurt it because I yelled. You can't let him play with these things. He can't tell the difference."

"I wasn't letting him play with it. He just grabbed it. But he'd let it go just as fast if you asked him nicely."

Riley wasn't sure what they were saying, but he liked the way Jeffrey said his part more. The only word he did understand was *Squirrel*. Squirrel was his favorite. He loved it more than anything. They'd been together since Riley was a puppy. He ran over to his dog bed in the corner to check on it. Good, right where he'd left it. He lifted it with his mouth and lay down.

His dog bed and Squirrel. Two of his favorite things.

"Look at him," Lisa said in a sweet voice. "That's right, Riley. You can have Squirrel." She looked at her brother. "*Not* the snowman. Which reminds me, Jeffrey, when we start setting up these Christmas decorations, you can't put any of the stuffed ones on a level Riley can reach. The plastic ones and the ceramic ones are fine, but not the stuffed ones." She opened the lid to her box and pulled something out. "And not cloth ones, either. Like this angel. Riley would tear this up and not think a thing about it."

"Mom already told me this."

"I'm just reminding you."

Riley kept hearing his name. They weren't calling him, so he stayed put. Lisa was nice to him sometimes, but other times she could become mean very quickly. She'd yell at him and say many things he didn't understand. He always responded by sending her calming signals, but she never seemed to pick up on his messages. Because of this, he was mostly nervous whenever she came around.

Lisa put the angel back in the box and closed the lid. She headed back up the stairs. "C'mon, Jeffrey. Stop playing with the snowmen. There's still a bunch more boxes to bring down."

"Okay." He got up and followed her.

Riley dropped Squirrel and was just about to follow Jeffrey up the stairs when he heard a familiar sound outside. His ears perked up. It was a car pulling in the driveway. Sounded like Dad's car. He barked to let everyone know and ran to the front door.

He barked several more times. Now a door closed. Footsteps on the sidewalk outside.

"Mom?" Jeffrey called, halfway up the stairs. "I think Dad just got home." He turned and headed back down the steps.

"Why's he coming home so early?"

"Riley," Lisa yelled. "Stop barking."

Riley heard keys jingling in the lock. It was the same sound he always heard. Had to be Dad. He backed out of the way, his tail wagging all the while.

Jeffrey reached the front door just as it opened. "Dad, it is you."

"It's me."

Lisa arrived and stood behind her brother. Riley heard more footsteps down the stairs. It was Mom.

"Tom," she said from the stairs. "What are you doing home so early? Is everything okay at work?"

"Look at the smile on my face," he said. "What's that tell you?"

Everyone seemed happy. Something good must be going on. Riley ran between their legs and began greeting Dad.

"Hey boy, how ya doing?" The father bent over slightly to pat his head. Riley kept jumping up on him, licking his hands and wagging his tail. "Okay, okay. Back up. Let me get through the door."

The mother walked up, hugged and kissed Dad. He closed the door then everyone walked to the middle of the living room. "I see you're getting the Christmas decorations out."

"Well, just the decorations for now," Mom said. "Remember? We talked about it this morning at breakfast? The kids and I would decorate the house this afternoon, then all of us would do the tree together tonight. But I thought I still had three hours."

"Well…" A big smile came over his face. "The plans have changed."

"Dad, what are you talking about?" Lisa said.

"We're not setting up the tree tonight?" Jeffrey said.

"No, we're not," Dad said. "Not tonight and not for about five more nights."

"What?" Mom said. "Tom, what's going on?"

"What's going on?" he repeated. "We're not decorating or setting up the tree tonight, *because*…tonight we have to pack."

3

"Pack?" Jeffrey yelled, startling Riley. "Tonight?"

"Why, Dad?" Lisa said. "We going on a trip?"

The father's smile got even bigger. "Yes, we are. And we need to leave first thing in the morning, which is why we have to pack tonight."

"What about our Christmas tree?" Jeffrey said.

"We'll have plenty of time to decorate the house and set up the tree before Christmas. In fact, this trip is all because of Christmas." He spread out his arms and gathered everyone toward the sofa. "Have a seat, and I'll tell you all about it."

Everyone sat down. Jeffrey sat in the middle, which Riley immediately interpreted as an invitation. He leapt onto his lap. He still didn't know what this was all about. He hadn't recognized a single word anyone said.

"Our CEO," Dad began, "asked everyone to meet in the lunchroom at one o'clock. Some of the hourly people looked pretty nervous thinking maybe this was going to be a layoff. But I knew it wasn't. Business has been great the last two quarters. Turns out, things were going even better than I realized. He said the Board decided to share the wealth, so everyone was going to get a significant Christmas bonus. In fact, they had the checks all ready. The bookkeeper was standing by the front door with a big box, ready to pass them out."

"Wow, Dad," Lisa said. "How much was it?"

"That piece of information belongs to your mom and I." He looked at her. "I will tell you when we're alone." He looked back at the rest. "Let's just say it was bigger than any Christmas bonus I've gotten since I started working there."

"Really, Tom?" Mom said.

He nodded. "And as soon as I opened the check and saw the amount, I instantly knew what I wanted to do with the money. My boss gave us the rest of the day off, but I stayed at my desk to work on my little Christmas present scheme. Took me just over an hour to iron out all the details. But everything came together and now—"

"Dad, would you just tell us already?" Lisa said. "The suspense is killing me."

"Okay. Here goes. You know how last summer we had planned a family vacation at Disney, but then we had to cancel?"

"Because it was too expensive," Lisa added.

"Yes," Dad said, "in a manner of speaking. And your mom really wanted to be able to stay at one of the Disney World resorts, not in a cheaper hotel twenty minutes away like we did the last time we went."

"Did we ever go to Disney before?" Jeffrey said. "I don't remember that."

"You were just a baby," Lisa said.

"Tom," Mom said, smiling, "are you saying—"

"That's exactly what I'm saying. I've already booked everything. It's all paid for. Tomorrow we'll get in the car and drive down to Disney World, where we'll stay for the next five days, with passes that will let us go to any one of the parks we want. Even different parks on the same day. And…we'll be staying at the Port Orleans French Quarter resort, which is right on the Disney property, less than five minutes from the parks. How's that sound?"

Everyone yelled and cheered at once. What was going on? Riley got off Jeffrey's lap, moments before he jumped to his feet. Jeffrey ran around the coffee table and threw his arms around Dad's waist. Lisa immediately did the same. Mom stood, walked around the table and leaned over the children to give Dad a kiss. They were all so excited and happy, which made Riley happy, too. Only he had no idea why. He stayed on the outskirts of the huddle wagging his tail, waiting for some direction.

"So, I'm guessing you approve," Dad said.

"Do we ever," Jeffrey said.

"The Port Orleans Resort," Mom said, "isn't that the one we were looking at on the internet?"

"Yes."

"Can we afford that?"

"We can now. I'm telling you, it's already paid for. The

rooms, the park tickets, the money for the food. The gas to drive there and back."

"I can't believe it," Mom said.

"Believe it. It's real."

Just then, before he'd even said anything, Riley detected a change in Jeffrey's mood. He watched as Jeffrey backed up and sat on the edge of the nearby recliner. Quickly, he rushed to be near him.

"But Dad, what about Riley? We can't leave him here all alone."

"What? No Jeffrey, we wouldn't leave Riley by himself."

Riley heard his name, twice. Now everyone was looking at him.

"Riley's going with us."

"To Disney? They let dogs go to Disney?"

"No, not at the parks. But there's a special kennel just for pets on Disney property, for people staying at the resorts. I looked it up online. It's huge."

"And," Mom added, "it's right down the street from Port Orleans, the Resort your father picked. That's one of the reasons I liked that resort so much. It's so close to the Disney kennel. We can stop and visit Riley whenever we want."

"Can we go every day?" Jeffrey asked.

She nodded. "As often as we want. They even have a nice fenced in play area. You and Lisa can take him out there for a run every day. The pictures on the internet looked really nice. The whole place is nice. I think he'll love it there."

Jeffrey squeezed Riley. "You hear that, boy? You're going with us to Disney."

"Which reminds me," Mom said. "Jeffrey, you need to get all his stuff together for the car."

"But Dad said we have to pack."

"You don't know how to pack," Lisa said.

"You just take care of Riley's stuff," Mom said. "I'll pack all your clothes. When you're done with that, pack your backpack with all the fun stuff you want for the car ride and the hotel."

"Okay."

"Well," Dad said, "let's get hopping."

"Wait," Mom said, "what about dinner?"

"I'll call the pizza place."

"Sounds good."

Riley watched Lisa run up the stairs and Jeffrey headed out toward the kitchen. He was just about to follow Jeffrey when Mom used his name. She was talking with Dad. He stopped in case he could understand anything else.

"Hey Tom, I just thought about another Riley detail. Did you ever go online to update his chip information for his tag? Remember we talked about it last summer when we thought we were taking the trip then?"

Tom's smile instantly disappeared. "No, I didn't. But I'll take care of it tonight."

"Tom...you better. It's over a year out of date. We moved since the last time it was active. Our contact information isn't the same anymore."

"I know. I'll take care of it."

Riley didn't know what either of them had said. They seemed a little tense. He ran through the kitchen trying to catch up with Jeffrey, but he had just left through the door leading to the garage and closed it behind him.

Oh, well. Better go check in with Squirrel.

4

Summerville Humane Society
Summerville, FL

Kim Harper, the Animal Behavior Manager and senior dog trainer at the shelter, sat in front of her computer screen reading everything she could about Dignity Pond, a new tiny-home housing complex set to open its doors shortly after New Year's Day. Its founder, billionaire Taylor Saunders, had asked to meet with Kim today. She had no idea why. The call hadn't come to her directly, but through the shelter's CEO.

Mr. Saunders could be arriving any minute.

The CEO had asked Kim to do whatever she could to accommodate the man, within reason. It's not every day a billionaire philanthropist comes knocking at your door. Like every other non-profit corporation, adequate funding was always an issue at the Humane Society. Her concentration was instantly broken when her office door swung open and a big hairy blur came bounding through.

"Finley, greet!"

Kim turned in her chair to welcome Finley, a mostly-golden retriever and one of her favorite dogs in the world. He instantly obeyed his owner Amy's command and sat right in front of Kim, eagerly waiting for her to respond. Amy Wallace was Kim's assistant dog trainer at the shelter. They'd started working together six months ago, after Amy's release from prison. While there, Amy had trained Finley as part of a program that prepared shelter dogs to assist war veterans struggling with PTSD. Finley had gone home with Chris Segar, a veteran of Afghanistan, who'd fallen in love with both Amy and Finley. He and Amy had recently gotten engaged.

Amy stood in the doorway.

"There's my beautiful boy," Kim said, scratching behind Finley's ears. "Oh, so soft." She ran her hands through his long reddish coat. "And silky." She gave him a hug. "And you smell so nice."

"He just got a bath," Amy said. "We're done for the day, right? After we do this private lesson?"

Kim looked at the clock on the wall then made a face. "That's why you're here." She had forgotten. She and Amy were supposed to be doing a private lesson together twenty minutes from now. Finley was supposed to come, too. "I'm afraid our plans have changed."

"What? What do you mean?"

"I got an assignment handed to me from the CEO a half hour ago. I'm supposed to meet with Taylor Saunders any minute. You know who that is?"

"I know he's a rich guy. I've seen him in the local news a few times. But why is he coming here?"

"I'm not exactly sure. Apparently, when he called he asked to speak with me, specifically."

Amy walked the rest of the way into the office and sat in a straight-backed chair. "So, we're going to have to reschedule the private lesson?"

Kim paused. She hated doing this but she knew Amy was ready. "Not exactly. I was thinking…"

"Uh-oh, what?"

"I'd like *you* to do the lesson."

"Me? You mean, without you?"

Kim nodded. "I really don't want to reschedule this lady. We had to postpone her last week, remember? When we had that little emergency in A-kennel?"

"I do, but…I've never done a private lesson by myself before."

"I know, Amy. And I'm not just asking you to avoid saying no to this lady again. The truth is, you are totally ready for this. This lesson is just about basic stuff. The dog is terrible on the leash. She goes nuts when other dogs walk by, and she jumps on everyone that comes in the front door. You can handle those kinds of things in your sleep. Besides, you've been teaching these behaviors in the group classes already. Not to mention all your training experience from the prison program."

"But all of those times were in a group. This will just be me and one owner. If I make a mistake it will really stand out.

22

What if she asks questions I can't answer?"

"Then you just say, *let me get back to you on that.* But there's a good chance you'll know the answer. You really are ready for this, Amy. I don't know if you've noticed this, but I've been letting you do more and more of the talking when we're doing private lessons."

"You have?"

"I have. On purpose. And you've been doing great."

There was a pause. Finally, Amy smiled.

"I'm serious," Kim said. "You will do just fine." Her phone rang. "I better get this. He might be here."

"Real quick," Amy said, "would it be okay if I called Chris and asked him to meet me at the client's house? He's already off work, and since part of the lesson is helping her dog behave better when dogs come around, I figure he could walk Finley for me."

"I don't have a problem with that. Sure. Tell Chris I said hi."

"I will." Amy called Finley, waved goodbye to Kim and headed down the hall.

Kim picked up the phone.

"Hey Kim, this is Anne out in the lobby. There's this really handsome, well-dressed guy who just walked through the front door. He's asking for you. Says he has an appointment?"

Kim decided it was probably Taylor Saunders. The man must be out of earshot, or else Anne would never say something like that.

"Do you want me to send him back?"

"No, I think I know who it is. And if I'm right, I'm expecting him. I'll come out there."

"Okay, I'll tell him. It's near the end of the day. Maybe hint that you're hungry. Judging by the wristwatch he's wearing, he could afford to take you anywhere in town."

"Just tell him I'll be right there." Kim hung up the phone and headed down the hall toward the lobby. There was a big mirror hanging in the hallway. Normally, she walked right by. For some reason, she stopped and checked herself over. Her hair, her makeup. Practiced a few smiles. She realized what she was doing and stopped.

Handsome, well-dressed billionaire.

Remember, he is just a man. Probably married. All the handsome, well-dressed ones were. When she reached the lobby, Anne saw her and waved. She pointed to where the man was sitting, at the end of a row of padded chairs reading a dog magazine.

Kim took a deep breath and tried to walk across the lobby as normal as possible. When she stood right in front of him, she extended her hand. "Mr. Saunders?"

He looked up and smiled. A very nice smile. "Mrs. Harper?"

"No, well…my name is Harper, but it's Miss. You can call me Kim, if you'd like."

"I'm sorry. I don't know why I assumed that you're married. Then please, call me Taylor." He stood and shook her hand.

He was quite tall. She noticed he wasn't wearing a wedding

band, either. "Okay…Taylor." It felt odd calling a man of his stature by his first name so soon.

"Thank you for seeing me on such short notice, Kim. I hope I didn't mess up your plans."

"You didn't. Just had to rearrange a few things. When my boss told me about your call, he didn't mention why you wanted to see me."

"That's probably because he didn't know. It's no big secret. I would have mentioned it, but I didn't make the call myself. My assistant did. Is there some place we could talk? It shouldn't take very long."

"Sure. We could either go back to my office, or maybe it'd be better if we met in our interview room. It's just down the hall."

"Great. You lead the way."

After Kim had taken a few steps, Taylor spoke up. "Say, I've got an idea. Don't feel you have to say yes, but I worked right through lunch and I'm kind of hungry. You have any plans for dinner?"

"No. Not really."

"Well how about this? We could go out and get a bite to eat, and I could share my proposal with you then."

"You have a proposal?"

"Kind of. I don't mean to make it sound so official. It's more like a big idea I've been thinking about lately. I'd like to run it by you, see if you think it's feasible. Something you might like to be involved with."

What in the world could it be? Was he thinking about

offering her a job? Her expression must have shown some confusion.

"It's an idea I'd like to explore. If it works, it would involve you, this shelter and my new project. You may have heard of it, Dignity Pond?"

"I have. I was just reading about it online before you arrived."

"Great. Well, that's what this little meeting is about. I'll tell you all about it over dinner. You want to drive in my car or follow me there?"

"Follow you where?"

"I was thinking of The Sierra House? Ever been there?"

Not in a million years, she thought. She couldn't afford the appetizers there. "No."

"I love that place. It'll be my treat."

"Well, I better follow you or we'd have to be back here by six. That's when they lock the front gate."

"Then you're right. We better meet there. Can you leave now?"

"Sure. I just need to go back to my office and get my things, turn off my computer. But wait, I'm not really dressed to eat at a place like that, am I?"

He stood back and looked her over, in a respectful way. "You look absolutely perfect. Besides, it's a pretty casual atmosphere there."

"Okay, if you say so."

"Know where it is?"

"Yes."

"I'll leave now and get us a table." He smiled, turned and headed out the front door.

Apparently, Anne had heard the entire exchange. She gave Kim a big smile and two thumbs up.

Eating at The Sierra House with a handsome, well-dressed billionaire. Not exactly the way Kim had imagined this day would end.

5

Kim pulled her nine-year-old Hyundai Santa-Fe into the parking lot of The Sierra House. The car, like her, seemed totally out of place. At least she had been able to change her shoes (she always kept a nice pair in the car). As she got out and made her way to the front door, she noticed almost every other car was either a BMW, Mercedes, Lexus, Cadillac or Audi.

She reminded herself how much none of this mattered. She got to work with dogs. Something she had wanted to do since she was a little girl. How many people can say that?

An attractive young hostess anticipated her arrival and held open the front door. "Welcome to The Sierra House."

"Thank you." She stepped into the foyer and immediately struck by the elegance. It resembled the lobby of an exquisite hotel. A large Christmas tree, fully decorated, filled the left corner. Another hostess stood behind a marble podium that was outlined in red and silver garland. "Do you have reservations?" she asked.

"I'm not sure. I'm meeting a man named, Taylor Saunders. I think he might already be—"

"Oh yes, Mr. Saunders. He's already here. He said to expect you. I'll take you to him."

"Great. Thank you."

"He comes here quite often," the hostess whispered. "He's such a nice man. The servers fight over who gets his table."

Kim didn't know what to say. She just followed quietly. They rounded a corner into the main dining room, divided into various sections by dark-paneled half-walls and slatestone pillars. The lights throughout were wrapped in shades, giving the place a warm, living room feel.

She continued following the hostess but noticed Saunders up ahead. He saw her, too, smiled and waved. As she reached the table, the hostess mentioned their server would be there in a moment to take their drink orders. Menus had already been set on the table.

"Thanks so much for doing this," Taylor said.

She sat. "You're welcome, but *this*…" she motioned with her hands about their surroundings, "…is hardly a sacrifice."

"No, I guess it's not. But still, I appreciate you getting with me so quickly. I'm flying to the UK first thing in the morning, and I was hoping to get this matter settled before then."

Kim was still so curious. She couldn't imagine what he had in mind.

"You said you were checking out the Dignity Pond website," Taylor said. "How far did you get in your search?"

"Not far," she said. "I read the homepage and began to

explore but got interrupted. I've seen some local news stories about it over the last month or two. Seems like a wonderful thing you're doing, especially for the homeless. You see a few homeless folks here and there in the downtown area, but it looks like your new housing complex can house up to forty people. Have you got that many people ready to move in?"

"Well, we still have room for a few more residents. But that's just for Phase I. We have plans for two more phases over the next two years. That is, if we can get all our approvals worked through. We're not just trying to reach the homeless living in the immediate area around Summerville but within a sixty-mile radius of the village. Last year we did something of an informal census and counted over fourteen-hundred homeless living within that circle. That's the year-round number. It's much higher in the winter."

"Really? That's...a staggering amount. Where are they all living now?"

"Lots of places. Mostly in the woods. Only a fraction actually live on the streets downtown."

The server walked up, introduced herself and asked what they'd like to drink. Taylor requested a glass of a specific brand of Merlot. He told Kim to feel free to order any wine on the menu. She declined. Instead, she ordered an unsweet iced tea with lemon. She had tasted some different wines before but had really only enjoyed a few. At the moment, she couldn't recall which ones.

"I still can't get over that number," she said. "Over fourteen-hundred. And here I am wondering if you'll get enough to fill forty beds. Now I'm wondering with that many, why you still have any openings. Seems like you'd have a huge waiting list of people wanting to get in."

"You'd think so, wouldn't you? One of the obstacles is the perception that they'd be giving up their freedom and be forced to live by a bunch of rules. The real sticky spot, though, is how few are willing to meet one of our main requirements."

"Which is?"

He held up his glass of wine. "No drinking. No drinking and no drugs. So many of them have been dependent on one or both for years. Some for decades. Our staff will provide all kinds of help for them to break free and stay free, if that's what they really want. But they have to want it. They have to come in totally ready to give it up and get clean. You'd be surprised how many aren't willing to do that, even for an opportunity like this."

"Wow, that's so sad."

"Very." He sighed, set his glass down and looked out the window. "But it's not something we can budge on. We don't really have any hope for lasting change if the substance abuse stays in place." He sighed again, looked at her. "Sadly, I know about this firsthand."

Did he have a history of drug or alcohol abuse? He seemed totally healthy and stable. If he did, why was he drinking that glass of Merlot? She wanted to ask what he meant, but wasn't sure that was an invitation.

"I can see you're wrestling with what I just said. I should explain. I'm talking about my father. He was an alcoholic. Not a violent one, thankfully. Moody and often depressed but, for the most part, he was kind. But it dominated his life. Well, our lives, too. My mom and me. That's my connection to all this. Why I'm funding the village." He set the glass down, looked out the window again. "Because of my dad's drinking, we wound up homeless. I spent my middle school years living in a tent in the woods."

"Oh my, Taylor. I'm so sorry."

"It gets worse. One winter, my mom got sick. I kept trying to tell my dad how sick she was, but he kept saying she'd be okay. But she wasn't. I knew she wasn't. By the time he finally broke down and agreed to take her to a hospital, it was too late. Her lungs were filled with fluid. She died of pneumonia the next day. Oddly enough, her death is what ended my life in the woods. The state got involved. When they found out where we'd been living, my dad lost custody of me. I entered the foster care system and we lost touch with each other. One summer during college, I went all over the state trying to find him." Taylor stopped talking a moment. Took a sip of wine.

"Did you? Did you find him?"

"In a manner of speaking. I found the last camp in the woods he'd been staying at. Some of the people who knew him told me what happened. He'd died two years earlier. Apparently he was crossing a dark road late at night on his way to a convenience store to pick up some more beer. He was struck by a truck and died instantly."

Kim could hardly believe what she was hearing. She had heard plenty of sad stories but wasn't sure she'd ever heard anything as sad as this. "I'm so sorry, Taylor. That must've been a terrible thing to have to go through alone."

"It was a terrible thing. But I wasn't totally alone. I had some good friends who helped me through it. They were Christians who went to this college youth ministry on campus. I started going with them, and on one of those meetings the lights turned on inside for me. I gave my life to the Lord, and I don't feel like I've ever been alone a day since."

Kim was a Christian also, but her conversion story was bland and ordinary compared to his. This news did introduce a bright spot to the conversation. Taylor's mood even seemed to lighten as he recalled this part of his story. "I guess now I completely understand why you'd want to get involved in building something like Dignity Pond."

He smiled. A tear welled up in his eye. He wiped it away with a linen napkin. "If it had been available back then when I was a kid, my mother might still be alive. I don't think we could have talked my father into going. But I know for a fact my mom would have gone. And if she had, that cold or flu, or whatever else made her sick that winter would have been properly treated, and she would've been fine in a week or two. Instead, I've had to live my whole life without her."

Kim was so touched by Taylor's story. She had an urge to reach out and comfort him but resisted. "Well, now that I understand what's motivated you to spearhead this project, I'm still not sure what kind of role you have in mind for me? I'm a dog trainer. That's what I do. How does that fit in with what you have in mind?"

He smiled. "Guess I have wandered pretty far off-subject." He looked over her shoulder. "But, we've been gabbing the last several minutes, and the server is headed back this way expecting to take our order. Let's figure out what we want to eat and after we tell her, I'll explain how you fit into the plan."

6

When the server returned, Kim ordered grilled salmon marinated in ginger and lime. Taylor ordered an aged, twelve-ounce oak-grilled New York strip, medium-rare. She tried not to focus on the prices, but it was hard. Her dish came close to the amount her parents had spent for all three of them when they had taken her out last week. "So…Taylor, you said you were going to tell me how your plans for this new Dignity Pond village involve me."

"Yes, I did. I got the idea watching a video on YouTube. It was all about that program you've been doing out at the prison. You know, the Prison Paws and Pals Program? I was fascinated by what I saw. I actually got choked up a few times, hearing about the impact these dogs are making in the lives of veterans with PTSD, and with the inmates, too."

"It's been an amazing project to be part of," she said. "There's really no downside to it."

Taylor took the last sip from his wine glass. The server noticed and came right over with a bottle, offering to pour another. He politely waved her off. "Never drink more than one." He looked back at Kim. Yesterday, I was given a tour of the program at the prison."

"Really?"

"The lady who directs the program, Captain Cummings—"

"Yes, Bridget. She's a good friend of mine."

"And she thinks the world of you. She kept talking about what a difference you made out there. Apparently, a few years ago someone else used to pick out the dogs. She said in almost every class back then a number of dogs had to be returned to the shelter. Now it's rare if any don't make it through and get adopted. She also said you completely changed the methods the inmates use to train the dogs, and the results have been amazing."

"She's being very kind."

"Maybe so, but it also sounds like you are one very gifted dog trainer."

Kim didn't know what to say. She got compliments about her dog-training efforts fairly often and always found them difficult to sit through. Time to change the subject. "So…you were going to say what you have in mind. For me, I mean."

The server came up with a basket of fresh bread and their salads. "I'll explain it in a minute." After the server left, Taylor asked if Kim minded if they prayed before eating.

"Not at all. I always do when I'm by myself."

"You do?"

She nodded.

He smiled, then said a quick prayer. He lifted the red cloth napkin covering the basket of bread. "Try the bread, by the way. It's *so* good."

She grabbed a slice and buttered it.

"I'm not sure if anyone else has tried this idea," he said. "I haven't had time to research the internet to see, but after meeting with Captain Cummings yesterday, I was pretty encouraged by the setup out there at the prison. I don't see why we couldn't make something like that work for us. That is, with your help.

I think the kind of people who are serious about coming out of the woods and getting back into mainstream society might experience the same benefits being with these dogs as our veterans do. I'm not thinking about you training the homeless to prepare dogs for vets, but for you to select dogs from your shelter who might actually live at Dignity Pond— with our clients—as companions."

"Like therapy dogs?" Kim said.

"Yeah. I guess that's the idea. After watching the video, I started looking at a bunch of others on YouTube. There's quite a few programs popping up around the country doing the same thing. And I kept hearing the same incredible results, one after another, about the difference these dogs are making in their day-to-day lives. I believe they could significantly improve the quality of life for the clients we'll serve at our village." He stopped talking for a moment. "What do you think?"

Hmmm. What did she think? "It sounds…feasible. I mean, I can see how something like this could work. I've never actually worked with the homeless before, but you seem to know plenty. I'm sorry, that didn't sound right."

"It's okay. I know what you mean."

She realized how odd it sounded, that a well-known billionaire was thoroughly acquainted with homelessness. "Can I ask you a few questions?"

"Sure. Anything."

"Are you thinking the dogs, if we provided them, would be owned by the clients themselves, or by the village?"

"I've actually thought a lot about that. Ideally, we'd like them to eventually become the pets of the clients they're helping. But I'm also very concerned that we do what's best for the dogs. Some of these clients might not be all that stable, especially at the beginning of their stay."

Kim was glad to hear him say this. "How long would you expect clients to live at Dignity Pond?"

"Up to two years. Our hope would be by then they are stable and ready to re-enter the real world, so to speak. Ideally, all those who come in will stay and make it all the way through. But I know that's not realistic. Because it's not, I'm thinking we would keep the dogs as residents of the village and, over time, clients would grow in their responsibilities with the dogs, and have opportunities to spend more and more time with them. Kind of like a probationary period, or something of a reward system. I haven't worked out all the details yet. Actually, I was hoping you could help me with that part."

Kim was liking this more and more. Of course, it would be her CEO's decision, but she thought he would love it. "Would you think, I mean down the road a ways, that if someone actually does make it all the way through, they'd be able to take a dog they've been working with home with them? Permanently?"

Taylor smiled. "Wouldn't that be a wonderful moment? To get to see something like that happen?"

"Definitely," Kim said.

"So, what do you think? Are you interested in helping us out?"

"Yes. We'll have to work out the details and all the practical stuff but, yes. I *love* your idea, Taylor. And I'd love to be a part of making it happen."

7

John carried a couple of good-sized logs from the wood pile back to the main fire. It was his turn to keep the evening fire going through dinner and into the early evening. For the better part of the day, he'd been able to avoid that cameraman making the documentary on the homeless. He'd arrived that morning just as breakfast was finishing up.

Alfred had said at first all but a few folks were avoiding him. But apparently, the guy disarmed everyone by the things he'd said, the questions he'd asked, and the way he'd asked them. Made everyone feel like he really cared, like he was only making this film to help change the public's perception about the plight of the homeless.

Maybe so, but John didn't trust him.

In his experience, few people genuinely cared about people like him. Some pretended to, while secretly pursuing their own agenda. He remembered one guy about five years back, who started out doing something similar. Made a video of a bunch of homeless people to use as a fundraising tool for a nonprofit corporation he planned to start. Turned out, he pocketed all the money he'd raised. Tens of thousands of dollars. Then disappeared.

John squatted down, let the logs fall to the ground beside the fire. He took a poker stick and made some room for the new logs then pushed them into place. The heat was pretty intense, causing him to back away quickly. It had warmed up today, as promised. John only wore a light jacket now, had his big leather one back in the tent.

"Don't look now, John, but that cameraman's headed this way." It was Alfred.

John looked over his shoulder. The guy was making a beeline for them escorted by Hampton, one of the two main guys who ran the camp. John was half-tempted to get up and run but that would be too obvious. He couldn't stay down here pretending to fiddle with the fire. It was too hot. He decided to sit in one of the chairs on the far side of the fire. "Don't you leave me here with him, Alfred," he whispered. "You sit here, too."

Two other people sat on the other side of the fire, the side closest to the cameraman. Maybe he'd set his sights on them. There was Jenny, a gal in her fifties who looked considerably older. John had seen her in different camps over the years and genuinely liked her. She had her tent site all done up for Christmas, including a decorated palm tree.

Sitting next to her was the Professor. John didn't know his real name. That's what everyone called him. It was clear he liked the nickname. He had a Master's degree from Harvard, or so he claimed. John had also heard him say he used to be a member of the Special Forces. He claimed he'd once played chess with, and almost beat, the legendary Bobby Fischer. And supposedly the Professor had written a great novel. Only one, mind you, and it was out of print now. But the year it came out, it had been a runner-up for the Pulitzer Prize.

Hampton walked up and introduced the cameraman, Mr. Lassiter, to everyone sitting around. "To your left is Jenny, a long-time resident of the camp. She's like a mother or sister to most of the guys here. Next to her is the Professor, one of our most educated residents. On the other side of the fire is Two-Sheets, about as easy-going a guy as you'll wanna meet."

"Two-Sheets?" Lassiter said. "Is that what you call him?"

"The name's Alfred. If you're gonna film me, I'd rather you use that."

"Okay."

"Beside him," Hampton continued, "is his good friend, John. John, I'm sorry, I forgot your last name."

Why did they need to know his last name? He didn't mention anyone else's last name. "Are you filming now?"

"Not yet," Lassiter said.

"Then it's Finch," John said. "But I'd really rather not be a part of your program, if that's all right."

"He's only trying to help us out, John," Hampton said. "I don't see the harm—"

"That's all right," Lassiter said. "I respect a man's privacy. But Mr. Hampton's right, John. I really am on your side. You know about YouTube, right? It's pretty much changed everything. Made a way for all kinds of people to become informed about things they never used to hear about. Like…well, folks like you."

"I've heard of YouTube," John said. "We don't get a very strong WiFi signal out here in the woods."

Alfred and Jenny laughed.

"No, I suppose you don't," Lassiter said.

Alfred leaned toward John. "Don't you need electricity for something like that?"

"If we get electricity out here," Jenny said, "we're going to plug in my Christmas lights first, before we hook up to the internet."

"Okay guys," Hampton said. "Mr. Lassiter knows we don't have things like electricity or the internet out here. He was just trying to make a point. That lots of people out there do." He pointed in the direction of the nearest road.

"That is what I meant," Lassiter said. "Before things like YouTube, the only exposure regular folk ever had about the homeless was the occasional story on the local news. Most of that was negative. Some homeless person getting hurt or beat up, or maybe causing some kind of problem downtown."

"Or embarrassing the politicians," Jenny added.

"Yeah," Lassiter said. "That, too."

"But now, some high school or college kid decides to do a term paper on the homeless, and what do they do? They google it. And right there on the first page, a few clicks away, are a bunch of YouTube videos they can watch. And when they do, wouldn't it be nice if they're being informed on the subject by a video like this one, the one I'm making? One that helps you all look like real people with real lives? Real stories, that matter? Hear about your hopes and your dreams?"

"Almost had me going until that one," Alfred said.

"What do you mean?" Lassiter said.

"Hopes and dreams? We aren't college kids out here, with our whole lives in front of us. Most folks are out here because their hopes and dreams imploded, or exploded. Take your pick."

"All right," Lassiter said. "Maybe that was a poor choice of words."

No maybe about it, John thought.

"I'm just saying, videos like this have a chance of making a difference. Maybe not with old-timers, people already set in their ways. But there's a new generation coming up who are getting most of their information from the internet. I don't know if millions of people will see it. But thousands will. And maybe when they do, the next time they see a homeless person something will click inside. They won't view them negatively, or just as bad, pass right by them as if they don't even exist." Lassiter got choked up saying that. "I'm sorry. Excuse me." He walked off, back toward the tarped area.

"What just happened?" Jenny said.

John watched Lassiter pull a paper towel off a roll on the table and wipe his eyes with it.

"I'm telling you guys," Hampton said, "this guy's for real. I heard him talk about it earlier today. Got choked up about it then, too. He's not doing this for the money. He's a retired

Army guy. Apparently an Army buddy of his came home from Iraq about five years ago, had PTSD real bad and got all messed up on drugs. He wound up being homeless in some city up north. Detroit, I think. Anyway, I guess this guy froze to death right out there on a city bench and people kept walking by him. Nobody realized he was dead for almost two days."

The look on everyone's faces instantly changed.

Even John felt that one in his gut. Nobody ought to go out that way, especially a man who fought for his country.

Maybe John should give this guy another chance.

8

Jeffrey was beside himself with excitement. Five minutes ago, they drove under the big, colorful arch across the road that announced they were now within the borders of Walt Disney World. His mother had read aloud the little blue banner underneath, "*Where Dreams Come True.*" Then Dad had announced, "Kids, for the next five days every place we go and everything you see will be a part of Disney World."

Both Jeffrey and Lisa squealed with delight.

They had just turned off the main road onto another road, then turned left again. "There's another sign," Jeffrey said. "Port Orleans Resort. The arrow's pointing straight ahead. See it?"

"I see it," Dad said. "I also see the GPS onscreen. It's right on this road."

They passed by an entrance to another resort on the right. The sign said: *Old Key West.* A minute later, they passed a sign that said: *Riverside Four Seasons Resort.* They drove past it also.

Lisa screamed, "Dad, stop the car. You just passed it."

He didn't stop.

"Dad, that was it. Didn't you see what it said on the iron gate? *Port Orleans, French Quarter.* I think that's the road we're supposed to turn on."

"Dad did see it," Mom said. She pointed to the GPS. "It says right there, that's the road, but we're not going there just yet. Did you forget someone?"

Jeffrey realized who they were talking about. "Riley?"

He had been asleep but woke up a few minutes ago when all the excitement began. Now his ears perked up, hearing his name.

"That's right," Dad said. "I told you one of the main reasons we picked the French Quarter is the kennel's right down the street. We'll stop in there, get him situated, then come back and check in at the resort."

"Did you hear that, Riley?" Jeffrey said, putting his arm around Riley's shoulder. "We're going to take you to a dog motel."

They drove on a minute or two more, past another entrance to the *Port Orleans Riverside Resort.*

"It's just up on the left," Dad said. A moment later, the GPS lady said the same thing.

"There it is," Lisa said. "*Best Friends Pet Care.*"

They pulled into the left turn lane, then left again into the facility.

"This looks nice," Mom said, as they parked the car.

"Okay, Jeffrey…you have Riley's leash?" Dad said.

"Yep."

"Gripping it like I showed you?"

"I am."

"Lisa, you grab his suitcase and let's go."

Riley followed Jeffrey out of the car. He loved riding in the car most of the time. But not *that* long. He had to go to the bathroom in the worst way. Seeing a patch of green grass off to his right, he began to pull in that direction trying to give Jeffrey a hint.

"Dad, Riley has to go."

"That's fine. It was a long car ride. We can wait."

Riley felt the leash go slack. It worked. He hurried over to the grass patch.

"Does anyone have a bag?" Lisa said, "in case he poops?"

"They should be in his little suitcase," Dad said.

"It's okay," Jeffrey said. "He's all done. Just went number one."

Relieved, Riley followed Jeffrey across a parking lot, up a curb and down a sidewalk toward some glass doors. Smells were everywhere. Whatever else was in this building, dogs were too. Lots of them. Now he heard barking coming from inside. He started to tense up but didn't sense any tension in the air. The mood of the entire family was very positive and upbeat. The family walked up to a counter on the left. The father was talking with an older woman. Jeffrey stood nearby, so Riley sat next to him.

"We have reservations for Riley. That's the name of our

dog. We're the Mitchell's from Savannah. I'm Tom."

"Hello, Tom. My name is Stella." She clicked a few keys on a keyboard. "Let's see, Riley. Yes, there he is. You're staying for five days?"

"Right."

"At the...*Port Orleans Resort*. That's right down the street."

"That's why we picked it," Jeffrey said. "That way we can come see Riley every day."

"That's right," Stella said. "You can come visit him as often as you want. Back up a minute. Let me see Riley."

Riley kept hearing his name, then Jeffrey stepped back from the counter.

"Oh, isn't he adorable. He looks just like Spot, from my first grade reader." She looked at Jeffery's parents. "Do either of you two remember that? No, you couldn't. You're too young. But I'm telling you, Riley is the spitting image of Spot." She looked down at Riley again. "See Spot run. Run Spot run." Then she laughed. "I'm sorry. No one gets my jokes around here."

A door opened on the left. A younger woman walked in. "Gina," Stella said. "These are the Mitchells from Savannah, and this is Riley. He'll be staying with us for the next five days. Will you show them around?"

"Sure. Oh, look at him. What a beautiful dog. Some kind of spaniel, right? Is he a King Charles Cavalier or a Springer?"

"We're not sure," Mom said. "We adopted him from a shelter. They thought maybe he was half of each. All we know is, he's a really great dog. Loves people, including kids. And other dogs, too."

"Then he'll love it here. Did you guys sign up for our Play and Stay program? It's especially for dogs that enjoy being with other dogs. They get to spend several hours a day playing together, with supervision of course."

"We already signed up for that," Lisa said.

"Great. Then I'll show you where he'll play each day," Gina said. "And show you his room."

"They booked him for an Indoor four-by-eight room," Stella said."

"Got it," Gina said. "Follow me folks."

"Why don't you guys take Riley on the grand tour," Dad said. "I'll stay here and take care of the paperwork."

"We'll be back in a few minutes," Gina said.

Riley wondered what was up. Nothing was making any sense. He hardly understood a single word being said. The only thing he knew for sure was, everyone still seemed quite happy. So this new place, though unfamiliar, couldn't be all bad. He watched as the young woman walked back through the door she had come out of, only this time everyone but Dad followed her. Including Jeffrey. So that meant, Riley followed too.

Jeffrey enjoyed the tour of the facility. It made him feel a little better about leaving Riley there while they were at Disney World. Especially the part about how close it was to their resort. But he didn't like the room Riley would be living in. It wasn't bad, but there was no way for him to go outside, unless someone brought him there on a leash. Back home, Riley loved to lie down outside in their backyard.

When they got back to the lobby area, Jeffrey's father said, "Everything's all set. Everybody say goodbye Riley. Jeffrey, why don't you give the leash to Gina, so she can take him back to his room?"

Jeffrey did what he was told. "Dad, couldn't we let Riley stay in the other room she showed us?"

"What other room?"

"The one where he can go inside or outside. Since he can't go to any of the parks with us, I think he should at least be able to be outside if he wants."

"You'll be able to take him outside," Dad said. "Whenever we come here to visit."

"I know, but that's just like once a day. Maybe twice. Gina showed us these rooms that have a patio. He can go out and in whenever he wants."

Dad looked at Stella, still standing behind the counter. "How much more is that per day?"

"Just a few dollars more. It's not that expensive."

"Do you have any more of those available?"

"Let me check." She typed some things into the keyboard. "Just one left open for the entire time."

"Okay, let's do that. Can you just put the difference on my card?"

"We can."

"Great. Then I think we're ready to go."

"Wait," Jeffrey said. "We forgot about Squirrel." He unzipped the bag they packed for Riley and pulled out Squirrel. "Riley needs Squirrel. It's his favorite thing. Can you make sure it gets in his room?"

"I certainly will," Stella said.

Everyone hugged Riley goodbye, except Dad who patted him on the head and scratched behind his ears. Jeffrey started to feel sad. He hated leaving Riley by himself, even at such a nice place. What would Riley think when they walked out the door? Wouldn't he think they were leaving him for good? He wished there was some way to explain what was happening to him.

"Jeffrey," his mom said. "Riley's going to be fine. He might be confused for a little while, but he'll cheer up when we come back to visit him. We can do that tomorrow right after breakfast, before we head over to the park. You'll see, he'll be fine."

"Okay." Jeffrey bent down and looked into Riley's eyes. "I love you, Riley. Don't be sad. We'll be back before you know it." He looked up at Stella. "You sure he'll be safe here? There's no way he can get out, right?"

"Riley will be perfectly safe the whole time he's here," Stella said. "You guys can go enjoy the Disney parks without any fear. Riley will be just fine. I promise."

9

As the family car pulled into the *Port Orleans French Quarter* entrance, Jeffrey tried to let the new, fun images of this happy-looking place erase the sad picture of Riley's face as they walked away, leaving him in the kennel by himself. Lisa had scolded him about not letting sad Riley thoughts ruin their family vacation. "Dogs aren't like people," she'd said. "Riley is having so much fun being in a totally different place, he's probably already starting to forget all about us being gone."

But what did she know? She hardly ever paid attention to Riley.

"Look at all the amazing Christmas decorations," Mom said from the front seat. They had just followed the signs to the parking area situated directly in front of the main lobby.

"Disney really does it up right, don't they?" Dad said.

Jeffrey looked. The building was very fancy. It reminded him of some of the older historic buildings back in Savannah. "Is this place old like back home?"

Dad turned off the car. "No, I think it's fairly new. It's just made to look old. They're trying to make it look like another old historic town called New Orleans."

Everyone got out. They each grabbed their rolling suitcase and walked toward the glass lobby area. It wasn't dark out yet, but Jeffrey could just imagine how fun it was going to be when they turned on all the Christmas lights. There were Christmas decorations everywhere he looked, even the pillars were wrapped in fancy garlands. They walked through the glass doors. Tall Christmas trees, with more decorations than Jeffrey had ever seen, stood in each corner of the lobby. In the center was a big water fountain. Set on each corner were large clay pots filled with bright red poinsettias.

"Isn't this nice?" Mom said. "Tom, I love this place already."

"How about we get checked in," he said, "put the bags in our room then come down to the food court for a quick bite to eat? Then we can catch a Disney bus over to the Magic Kingdom. If I timed this right, we should arrive there just about the time they turn on all the Christmas lights."

"I can't wait to see that," Lisa said.

"Will we have any time to go on any rides tonight?" Jeffrey asked.

"Probably," Dad said. "We'll have to check how late the parks are open."

"Your plan sounds great" Mom said, "with one minor change. Let's don't just dump the bags in the room and leave. Can we take two minutes to hang up the clothes that get wrinkled? I don't want to be doing any ironing on this trip."

"Sure, Hon. There's the front desk. I'll be back in a few minutes."

Jeffrey followed his mom and Lisa toward a green wooden bench. He sat and looked all around the lobby then through the glass back wall toward the rest of the resort. This had to be the fanciest place they'd ever stayed. Where Riley was staying was nice enough for a kennel. But this place was so much nicer. He wondered if dogs even cared about things like Christmas decorations. People acted like they didn't. But maybe they did. How would anyone know?

One thing Jeffrey did know, Riley sure liked opening up his present every year on Christmas morning. They'd wrap something special just for him and put it under the tree. He would always get so excited when they told him it was his turn. He'd find it, drag it out from under the tree and tear off the wrapping paper with his teeth. There was no way to be sure, but to Jeffrey, he seemed as happy as any of them opening up their presents on Christmas morning.

Riley was all alone and in a strange place.

Some kind of small room or pen. The only things he recognized were Squirrel and Monkey. Back home, he never cared much for Monkey. But here he mattered. Monkey smelled like home.

He looked around. Didn't seem like a bad place. The bed he was lying on felt comfortable enough. There was a bowl of water over in the corner. A nice little door that led to an outdoor area.

But why had they brought him here? Where was Jeffrey and the rest of the family? He thought back to when they'd left him a short while ago. Up until then, everyone had been happy. He thought they were just visiting this place. They had taken him on a walk throughout the building and outside. He'd walked past dozens of dogs, all shapes and sizes. There were lots of conflicting smells, but the few signals he was able to pick up on weren't very alarming.

He sensed some anxiety and confusion. Some loneliness, too. But many of the dogs seemed calm and content, especially the ones rooming with other dogs. The best part of the tour was…no one had lunged at him or threatened his safety. There wasn't any food in his bowl, but he felt certain food would be coming. He had smelled some in the bowls as he passed by.

He glanced over at Squirrel and Monkey, both lying beside him. They seemed fine for now, so he got up and headed out the little opening to the patio area. He walked to the edge of the cage and looked beyond the mesh for any traces of his family. They weren't anywhere. He couldn't smell them, either, except from memory.

But they would come back, wouldn't they? They always came back. Sometimes they left him at home for long periods of time. And just when he'd start to worry he'd never seen them again, he'd hear the car pull into the driveway, then that wonderful sound the garage door made. And the best sound of all, the keys jingling just outside the door.

Riley walked back through the opening, took a few laps of water then lay down on the bed. He grabbed Squirrel in his mouth and brought him closer. Maybe it was the exhaustion from the car ride or all the excitement of this new place, but he was feeling pretty tired.

Maybe in his dreams, he'd be with the family again.

10

As the monorail stopped at the entrance to the Magic Kingdom, Jeffrey tried to shed the annoying feeling he'd picked up a little while ago at the resort. After eating at the food court they had waited over thirty minutes for the bus to take them on a five-minute ride to the park. His sister Lisa complained that they could have walked the distance sooner.

Dad rebuked both of them for being so whiny, and said for the next five days they had better get used to waiting in lines. "That's what the Disney experience is all about. Incredible scenery, incredibly long lines, followed by the most incredible five-minute rides and attractions to be found anywhere in the world."

As they walked down the ramp from the monorail, they were being treated to some of that incredible scenery Dad had mentioned. The delay had brought them here just in time to see the Christmas lights turn on all over the Magic Kingdom. Ooo-s-and-ahh's filled the early evening sky.

"My gosh," Mom said, "would you look at that?"

They stopped walking to take it in. Jeffrey had never seen anything like this. It was unreal. He had seen similar scenes watching Disney movies or on the Disney channel. But seeing them up close with your own two eyes…there was no comparison.

"Guys, we gotta get a picture of this," Dad said. "I know we just got here, and I know I said I wasn't going to do this all the time, but…look at this. How can we just walk right by it?"

Lisa groaned. Mom made a face. She wasn't buying it. Jeffrey had heard them talk about this before. Really after every trip they ever took. *You take way too many pictures, Tom…I'm capturing memories, Hon.* Jeffrey didn't care either way. It was kind of fun to see Dad so excited, like he was a kid.

Dad got them all standing in the right position and at just the right angles, then pulled out a special folding tripod he'd purchased for this trip (after learning Disney didn't allow selfie sticks). He set the timer, snapped his smartphone into place then ran into position beside Mom.

"Smile, everyone." A flash. Then a quick run around to make sure the picture worked. "Perfect." He had everything back in place in less than two minutes. "See? That didn't hurt a bit." He kissed Mom on the cheek and off they went, past a giant Mickey Mouse head spread across a hillside made with red poinsettias. They walked through a tunnel under the Main Street Railroad Station and came out the other side on the Main Street square. An even more dazzling site. A Christmas Wonderland. A five-story tall Christmas tree served as the centerpiece, lit up with bright blue, green and red lights.

Golden garlands draped across the branches. Giant wrapped presents were stacked around the base.

"Oh, guys," Dad said. "We gotta get this one. C'mon. A quick family pic."

"Dad, no," Lisa said.

"Tom, really? We haven't even walked fifty feet into the park."

"But look at this site. Have you ever seen anything like it? It's like walking into a dream."

"It is beautiful, but can't you just take a quick pic with your phone? Do we have to get the tripod set up every time?"

"Not every time. Just some of the time."

"Dad," Lisa said, "Can't you just download Disney pics from the internet for your family slide show, so we don't have to stop every two minutes? For scenes like this one anyway."

"It's not the same, Lisa."

"It kinda is. Since we're seeing these things for real, it'll be just like you took them."

"No it won't. None of us would be in them."

"How about this for a compromise?" Mom said. "For some of the pics, you just use your phone, not the whole tripod set up. And settle for having just one of us in each pic. Then every once in a while, we'll do the whole family pic thing? How's that?"

"I guess that's okay."

Jeffrey remembered why Dad wanted everyone in the pics. Last year after their grandparents came to visit, Dad gathered everyone together for one of his trip slideshows. Toward the end Grandma had said, "Tom, how come we don't ever see you in any of the family pictures?" He double-checked and discovered that on the last four family trips he wasn't in a single photograph.

"Here," Mom said, "You can take one of all three of us, with the big tree in the background. Or better yet, I'll take one of the three of you, so you're in the picture."

Dad seemed okay with that.

As they took the picture, Jeffrey was a little distracted. Across the street, a crowd was forming in front of a little covered walkway. A moment later, he saw why. "Look, it's Donald Duck and Pluto. Right there. Can I get a pic with them? Maybe get their autograph?"

"Aren't you a little old for that?" Lisa said. "You know that's not really them, right? There's a guy in that suit, maybe even a girl. Disney will hire either one if they're the right height. I read an article about how hot it gets for people in those costumes. In the spring and summer months, they can only interact with people for twenty minutes at a time, or they'll drop dead."

Why was she saying all these things? Was it, like, her job to spoil everything for him?

"Lisa, just stop," Mom said. "I can recall you being here at Jeffrey's age pitching a fit every time you saw a Disney character. '*Oh, Mom, look it's Minnie and Mickey. Oh, Mom, there's Chip and Dale. Can we go see them? Huh? Can we?*'"

Jeffrey especially liked the way Mom tried to make her voice sound like Lisa's. It had the intended result. Lisa backed off.

"So, can we see them?" he asked.

"Not this time, Jeffrey. Tomorrow we'll figure out where the characters are located, and you and I will see them together, while Dad and Lisa go on a fast ride." She stopped walking for a second. "Can we all walk all the way down Main Street, just one time, without stopping to take a pic or standing in line for anything, and just take in all these amazing lights and sights and sounds and smells. Nice and slow. Then, when we're standing in front of Cinderella's castle, we'll turn around and see the whole street from that direction, all lit up. How's that sound?"

"Sounds great," Lisa said, "But can't we at least stop once before we take this magical walk of yours down Main Street? I gotta go to the bathroom. Like, really bad."

11

Everyone had pretty much finished eating dinner. As a rule, people cleaned up after themselves around here. John was glad of that. He'd been in some camps where they over-organized everything, including making people take turns cleaning up other people's messes after meals. That happened, he'd stay long enough to do his turn so nobody'd ever say John Finch didn't pull his weight. Then he'd up and leave the next morning.

He didn't choose to live out in the woods all these years to have some stranger telling him what to do all day long. He was okay with this assignment, taking turns tending the fire. With everyone joining in, you only got tapped for the task once every few days. The rest of the time was yours to do with as you please. There was certainly a long list of downsides to being homeless, but if there was an upside, John felt it must be that.

Freedom. No one telling you how to live. No one bossing you around.

"It's John, right?"

The unfamiliar voice came from behind. John had just finished resetting the fire in the pit. Turning, he saw it was the camera guy. What was his name again? "Yes, John."

"I'm getting ready to head out, John. Thought I'd take another stab at seeing if I could interview you. We could do it off-camera and I could still leave your name off of it. I could just say, '*I was talking with one of the men who lives at the camp, who'd rather not be interviewed on camera.*' Something like that. Then summarize some of the things you said. Would that work?"

John backed up and sat in his chair. "I've been doing some thinking. I guess I'm okay if you want to interview me. As long as I get to decide at the end if there's anything I want you to take out. You okay with that?"

"More than okay. That would be great."

"Alright. Where do you want to do this?"

"How about here? It's starting to get dark out. The light from the fire would help the picture quality."

John looked around. It was just the two of them, but that wouldn't last long. This was the main fire in the camp. "I've got a decent lantern in my tent. On its highest setting, gets pretty bright. I'd feel more comfortable talking if we're alone. People could start showing up here any minute."

"Why don't you lead the way, and I'll follow?"

John took one more look at the fire, making sure it would be fine for a while, then headed for the tent. As he walked, it dawned on him how silly it was to worry they might be overheard if they talked by the fire. This guy was about to make a video and put it on the internet. Thousands of people could watch this video once he uploaded it. But it felt different for John somehow.

Then he realized why. Nobody here had access to the internet. Heck, they didn't even have access to electricity. There was zero chance John would ever meet the people who might hear what he said to this guy. That's why it felt different. But still, he had to be careful. Some of his extended family members—people he hadn't connected with in years—might be on the internet. This wasn't the way he wanted them to see him after all this time.

Maybe he shouldn't do this after all.

He reached his tent. The guy was right behind him. Better just do it. Told the guy he would. Just had to make sure he didn't say too much. He bent down, unzipped the tent and reached for the lantern. "We can sit in these chairs." There was one on either side of the tent opening. "This one's mine, that one's Alfred's. Not sure where he is at the moment."

"I carry this chair around with me," the man said, lowering a strap attached to a canvas foldup chair off his shoulder. "Maybe I'll just sit in this. That way, if Alfred shows up he can sit in his own chair."

"Either way," John said. "He shows up, I'm okay with it. Nothing I wouldn't want to say around him. Alfred knows me better than just about anyone."

"Great. Just give me a minute to get set up. I'll put the camera on this tripod and set it between us, so that we're both in the frame. Not a very high-tech operation here."

John decided he better ask. "What's your name again? I know I already heard it earlier today, but I forgot."

"It's John, like yours. But my last name is Lassiter. Might as well just call me that. Everyone else has all day, and it will avoid any confusion while we're talking since we both have the same first name."

"Should I call you Mr. Lassiter?"

"Lassiter is fine. Mister sounds too formal."

"Okay...Lassiter." John took a seat. "Start asking away whenever you're ready."

"I will. And just say *I'd rather not go into that*, if I ask you a question you think is off-base."

This guy, Lassiter, did seem awful easy to get along with. A few moments later, he was all set to go.

"We're recording now. I'm just going to leave it running and edit later, so we can have a more normal conversation."

"Where do you want to start?"

"Well, there is one thing that kind of stands out when I talk to you, John. Compared to all the other people I've talked to so far. Not just at this camp today, but in other camps I visited while making this video."

"What's that?"

"I'm not exactly sure how to say this..." He looked around as if to confirm they were still alone. "Whenever you talk, unless you're extremely good at covering it up, you don't sound...even a little sloshed. Almost everyone else I talk to— and they're real upfront about it—is either a little high, a little drunk, or a little of both."

"And as the day goes by," John added, "maybe not a little."

"Right. That seems to be a pretty consistent issue out here, among the homeless I mean."

"Having a problem with alcohol?"

"Or some other substance abuse, yes. But you seem, I don't know, totally straight."

"That's because I am. Now, anyway. And for the last..." How long had it been, he wondered. "I guess almost four years, I've stayed sober. But that's not how I used to be. Used to be like everyone else, start drinking fairly early in the day, keep the buzz going throughout the day and, depending on how the day went, get totally hammered at night. Or if it was a good day, just drink enough to help me sleep. Either way, drinking was at the core of every day."

"Well, congratulations then."

"On what?"

"Being sober four years. How'd you stop, if you don't mind me asking?"

"Wasn't easy. But it was pretty much do it or die. I caught a cold one winter that moved into my chest. I was in a town that had a walk-in clinic, so I stopped in, see if they could give me something before the cough got much worse. Next thing I know, they're running all these tests on me. I'm telling them, 'You know, you'll never get your money back for all this.' They said, don't worry about it."

"What did you think was going on?"

"I had no idea. A few hours later, a doctor sits me down, looks me straight in the eye and says, 'Mr. Finch, I'm sorry to have to tell you this, but your liver's in bad shape. It's right at the point of no return. In fact, it might already be past that point. No way to know for sure without an MRI and a biopsy. But I can tell you this for certain. If you don't stop drinking, and I mean very soon, you are going to die. And I don't mean a few years from now. I mean, you might not be here this time next year.'"

"I guess that got your attention."

"It did. But in a way I didn't expect."

"What do you mean?"

"Up to that point, I was pretty sure I wanted to die. Thought about it pretty often. Anyone asked I'd have told 'em so. You'd think I'd welcome news like that. But instead, I discovered it bothered me. And not a little. A lot. Maybe I just didn't want to go out that way. Whatever it was, it gave me the edge to work harder at letting it go. The drinking, I mean. How I managed to finally pull that off is another long drawn-out story."

"I'd love to hear it if you don't mind sharing it."

John thought about it. He did mind. It had been the darkest and worst season of his life. He'd barely survived. It was so bad that when he finally did come out on the other side, he knew he'd never take another drink again. Nothing was worth going through that again. "What was that thing you said I should say?"

"What?" Lassiter said.

John remembered. "I'd rather we not go into that."

12

Last night, the Magic Kingdom had been so much fun. Dad had decided once they'd gotten there they might as well stay until the park closed. It stayed open longer than usual because of the special Christmas events. Jeffrey didn't know which of the two he liked better, the nighttime Christmas parade or the holiday fireworks. Both were so amazing; he couldn't imagine anything else topping them the rest of the trip.

Lisa, of course, liked Cinderella's Castle the best. It was all lit up like the theme from the movie *Frozen*, part of a holiday show called *Castle Dream Lights*. It was nice but after seeing it all lit up for a few minutes, Jeffrey was ready to go on some rides. They did get to go on some of the smaller attractions, but since they hadn't planned on staying all evening, Dad hadn't gone online to set up any *FastPasses*. For the big rides, and the most fun ones, without a *FastPass* you had to wait between forty-five minutes to an hour at each one.

But starting today, Dad had booked three *FastPasses* per day for the most popular rides. He warned them to expect some pretty long lines at the rest, because Disney only let you select three a day.

Right now, Jeffrey was standing outside their room at the *Port Orleans French Quarter* resort, leaning on a rail on the second floor, watching a boat go by down the narrow river that ran behind the hotel. He was waiting for Dad to come out. The girls were taking way too long getting ready, so Jeffrey had asked if the two of them could go visit. Riley. They'd arranged with the kennel to be there each morning to take him on his morning walk.

The hotel door opened. Jeffrey turned. "Are we going now?" His father smiled and held up the car keys. That meant yes.

"You remember how to get from here to the parking lot?" Dad asked.

"I think so. It was kind of dark out when we came back here." Their room was in the building at the far end of the resort.

"Well, lead the way. I'll help if you make a wrong turn."

His dad always did this when they went out together. Said it taught Jeffrey life skills. They rounded the corner and Jeffrey saw the elevators up ahead. "Elevator or stairs?"

"Elevators are for wimps."

"We took the elevator yesterday when we first got here," Jeffrey said.

"Elevators are for wimps and families with luggage."

Jeffrey laughed and headed down the stairwell.

"How'd you sleep last night?" Dad asked.

Jeffrey had to sleep on the rollaway bed. "Pretty good. I thought for sure I'd have all kinds of amazing Disney dreams after seeing all those things last night."

"But you didn't?"

"I don't think so." Jeffrey reached the bottoms of the stairs. "Like every other night, I don't remember a thing."

"So you had a good time last night at the park?"

They started down the long cobbled walkway that led to the front of the resort. "So much fun, Dad. I can't believe we get to be here all week. Which park are we going to do today?"

"Animal Kingdom. Hopefully, by the time we get back from visiting Riley the ladies will be ready to go."

They walked in silence a few moments.

"Whatcha thinking about?"

"Riley," Jeffrey said.

"What about him?"

"I just hope he's having as much fun as we are."

Riley really had to go.

He'd slept pretty well through the night. All his dreams were pretty much normal. So much so, that when he awoke he was surprised not to find himself at home. Instead, everything was instantly and totally unfamiliar. Then he remembered. The family dropped him off at this place yesterday.

Last night, a nice lady had given him food and changed his water bowl. She had come back a little while later to take him for a walk, so he could do his business. Was she coming back again?

He needed her to. He didn't want to go in the little area outside, but he might have to if someone didn't come pretty soon.

He strained his eyes to get a glimpse down the aisle, just outside the front of his pen. Should he bark to get someone's attention?

Just then a door opened. Footsteps. He couldn't help himself. He barked for all he was worth. Then he saw her, a different lady dressed much the same way. He barked some more and pranced in place. She was coming. Even better, she had a leash in her hand.

"Riley, is that you making all that noise? You have to go out boy? I bet you do." She was standing in front of him now. "Guess who's here to see you? It's Jeffrey. He's gonna take you for a walk. So, you sit so I can put this leash on you."

Riley was beside himself. He picked up four words of that. All of them good. *Out...Jeffrey...walk...sit*. He backed up and sat for her, but he could barely keep still. Took her several times, but then he heard that wonderful click.

"Okay, Riley. Let's go see Jeffrey."

They walked down some hallways past a number of other dogs in kennels. Some barked, some just watched, some just looked up as Riley walked by. His attention was focused forward, eyes scanning everywhere looking for just one person.

There he was—Jeffrey.

"Riley!" Jeffrey hurried in his direction.

Riley strained his neck at the end of the leash. A moment later, Jeffrey was hugging him and getting licked all over in return.

"See, I told you we'd come back. Want to go for a walk? A walk?" He looked at the worker. "Has he been out yet?"

"Nope. We were waiting for you. As you can see, he's all ready to go. Follow me, and I'll show you where you can take him."

Riley, Jeffrey and his dad followed the worker out to a large dog park where several dogs were already running around and having, what looked to Jeffrey, like a fun doggy time. She showed them the beginning of a special trail created just for dogs and owners to enjoy.

"You can either let Riley run loose in the fenced area, or keep him on the leash and walk him around the trail. Or you can do both, one after the other. It's totally up to you. You just have to stay with him the whole time and clean up after him if he poops."

"I think we'll take him on the trail. Is that okay, Dad?"

"Sure. How long is it?" he asked the worker.

"Not long. A few minutes."

"Okay then, Jeffrey. You lead the way."

They said goodbye to the lady and headed down the trail. As soon as they reached the first patch of grass, Riley quickly stopped to go the bathroom. Fortunately, it was just number one. But Jeffrey knew from all the walks at home, in less than five minutes he better be ready with that poop bag. He hated cleaning up after Riley. Dogs had to go, and when they did, they went outside. He got that.

The problem was, Riley would be walking along just fine, then suddenly stop and squat, but then he'd keep walking in that awkward-looking pose, dropping pieces of poop as he went. If you were lucky, they picked up easily. When Riley was nervous, like he would surely be this morning...

Well, it was just an awful thing.

13

Later that day, Jeffrey and his dad had waited in a thirty-minute line at Disney's Animal Kingdom's *Dinosaur* attraction. Mom and Lisa were waiting in an even longer line for a spinning roller coaster ride called *Primeval Whirl*. Lisa loved rollercoasters as much as Jeffrey hated them.

They had been together just before lunch when they'd used their first *FastPass* of the day for the *Kilimanjaro Safaris* attraction. So far, that had been Jeffrey's favorite ride at the park. They rode through this big tract of land, made to look like an African savanna, in an open-air, half-bus/half-jeep vehicle. All the animals were right out there in the open, just like you'd see on the nature shows on TV.

In fact, at one point their safari vehicle had to wait five minutes because a rhinoceros decided to just stand there in the middle of the road. It stared at them for a while, then looked away. Eventually, it moved on. Jeffrey wouldn't have minded if the wait had lasted even longer. He'd never seen a rhinoceros before, let alone one up close like that.

He saw giraffes, elephants, zebras and ostriches all walking around out in the open. A bunch of hippos swam around in a pond. He saw some crocodiles, too. Even a lion with a full mane, laying up on a rock. Dad said the lions weren't actually loose like the other animals. For obvious reasons. They were in a big pen made to look like they were free, but it was circled by a wide moat that kept them from going after their own food.

The safari ride was just over twenty minutes long. Jeffrey wished when they had gotten off, they could get right back on again. "Dad, how long is this Dinosaur ride?" They turned a corner in line and started walking down a row just as long as the one before.

"Don't ask."

"Why? I want to know."

He took out his smartphone, tapped the screen a few times. "Three minutes."

"That's all?"

"Yep, three minutes. That's why I said, don't ask. But hey, this is a way better deal than that tilt-a-whirl ride your mom and Lisa are going on. Their line is forty-five minutes, but the ride is only half as long as ours."

"A minute-and-a-half? That's all how long their ride is?"

"Yep." They walked a few feet further. "It's crazy that we all do this. Over and over again, all day long."

"Day after day," Jeffrey said. "Every day we're here. Except for the *FastPass* rides. Those aren't bad at all. How come they don't let you do *FastPasses* for all the rides?"

His dad looked down at him. "I could answer that, but I want you to think a minute. See if you can figure out why."

Jeffrey thought. Then it hit him. "If all the rides were *FastPass* rides, everyone would use them for every ride."

"And then what would happen?"

"None of the lines would be fast. All of them would be long."

"Right."

"Hey, Dad." Jeffrey pointed forward. A gap had formed while they stood there talking. His dad quickly filled it before anyone behind them got annoyed. And they would, too. It was almost a crime at Disney, not keeping up your place in line.

They didn't talk for a few minutes, just kept moving forward a few feet every other minute or so. Jeffrey thought about Riley and how much fun it had been seeing him that morning. After taking him on the nature trail, Dad said Jeffrey could turn him loose in the dog park a few minutes, so he could get some exercise. Riley loved to be around other dogs, and he instantly connected with a corgi and a poodle. In seconds, they were running around together, jumping and chasing each other, tails wagging like crazy.

"I wonder what Riley's doing now?"

"Huh?"

"Riley, I wonder what he's doing now, at the kennel. If he's having any fun."

His dad looked at his watch. "He might be. I forgot to ask what time they do it, but at some point they're going to let him run loose in that dog park with all the other friendly dogs.

For several hours, I think the gal said."

"Really?"

"Yep. Paid extra for it."

"Thanks, Dad. I'd feel bad if he was just sitting there all day in that kennel by himself."

"Me, too. But he'll probably have a total blast then be wiped out for the rest of the day."

"Too bad he couldn't come here with us."

"He wouldn't like it here. What would he do all day? Stand in line for hours and hours, like us? And then what? He couldn't even go on the rides. Have you seen those signs in front of each ride that measure how tall kids have to be before they can ride? He's not tall enough for any of them."

"No, I guess not."

"Even if they did let him on the rides, he wouldn't have any fun. He'd bark his head off at everything. This ride we're about to go on would scare him to death. All those dinosaurs lunging at him from out of the darkness. He'd totally freak out."

Jeffrey laughed. He could just see it. When Riley got scared, he didn't just bark. He made this high-pitched squealing noise that almost sounded like a woman's scream. And while he was screaming, he'd get this terrified look in his eyes.

"No," Dad said. "Riley's better off where he is. Besides, dogs have a different way of passing the time than we do. You ever notice how much he sleeps? He must take, like, five naps a day. And then when it's bedtime, he's just as tired as we are, and sleeps all night. How is that possible? If I take a thirty minute nap during the day, it messes up my sleep for the whole night."

All this definitely made sense. Jeffrey didn't feel so bad anymore. "Can we go back and see him tonight before we head back to the room?"

"Sure. But did you remember, tonight we're going in that hot tub together? Remember the one we passed by this morning on our way to the food court? I think your mom and I will need to soak in that thing after walking for so many hours."

"Can't we do both? See Riley and do the hot tub?"

His dad thought a moment. "I suppose. I guess you and I can drop the girls off at the lobby, so they can get ready for the spa first."

"Then you and I can go visit Riley."

"Alright. We'll do that."

"Uh, Dad?" Jeffrey pointed.

"What? Oh." He quickly closed the gap between them and the couple in front. He leaned over and whispered, "Just think, only fifteen more minutes of this and we get to go on our three-minute ride."

14

John, Alfred and Jenny warmed themselves by the fire. John had just moved back a few feet. The bottom of his feet were getting too hot. The cold snap of the last few days had definitely ended. It was a pleasant forty-nine degrees out. The high today was only fifty-two, though John was pretty sure they wouldn't see it. It had been sunny all morning and through the afternoon, but the overhead sky had begun to grow dark in the last few minutes.

John had lived long enough in Florida to recognize what came next. A thunderstorm. The only question was how bad it would be and how long it would last. You could never tell in Florida. Some of the meanest and darkest looking clouds turned out to be nothing. Others that looked fairly harmless wound up throwing down Zeus-sized lightning bolts and dumping several inches of rain.

A long, low rumble. Behind them. That's where most of the storms came, from the west.

"There it is," Alfred said. "Won't be long now."

"Maybe not," Jenny said. "It might blow over."

"Wanna bet? 'Cause I'm pretty good at detecting these things."

"You are, eh?"

"I am. I can tell by how long that rumble lasted, it's coming here for sure. I'd say…five minutes, maybe a few minutes more. But that's it."

"I'd take that bet, but I got nothing to bet with. Ran outta cash yesterday."

"Well, then let's just shake on it." Alfred reached out his hand. Jenny shook it.

Another rumble. Deeper, louder.

"I think Alfred's gonna win this one, Jenny," John said. He stood up and glanced at the sky through the trees. "Wow, look at that."

Alfred and Jenny got up and turned around. At the westernmost edge of the woods the sky almost looked like nighttime had set in.

John started to feel a tinge of fear. For all the advantages Florida offered the homeless, it was also known to be the lightning capital of the U.S. It was no fun living outside when one of these electricity-filled storms blew through your camp.

"You win," Jenny said. "I take back my bet." She started walking away. "Better get my tent site ready. I hope it's just rain and not a lot of wind."

Alfred looked at John. "Maybe we should get ready, too."

John realized, this would be the first thunderstorm he'd experienced at this camp. He followed Alfred back toward their site, all the while looking up at the trees. So many of them.

So many targets.

As soon as they reached the tent, they started undoing the clothespins and dropping their clothes into laundry baskets. They were still wet from being washed that morning.

"Guess it'll be another inside-out day tomorrow," Alfred said, referring to his underwear situation. "With this storm coming, no chance these'll get dry."

"It's been nice wearing clean *and* dry clothes the last few weeks," John said. That was made possible by the long string of days without rain. Some weeks in Florida it rained every afternoon, like clockwork. That happened, you either wore your clothes dirty for a while or hauled your laundry downtown by hand, to the nearest laundromat.

John smiled as he thought about it. He had never seen Alfred in a laundromat before, didn't know if Alfred had ever set foot in one.

A brilliant FLASH, then BOOM!!

John dropped to the ground, covered his head. What just happened? Was he okay? Did he just get struck? He froze a moment and took stock. Didn't feel numb. Wasn't in any pain. He could feel his heart pounding in his chest.

"John? You, okay?"

"I think so. You?"

"Yeah, think so. But, man. That was close."

"Too close." John sat up, then stood. He was still shaking inside.

"Wouldn't have even gotten to one-Mississippi on that one." Alfred always did that during thunderstorms. Counted one-Mississippi, two-Mississippi, three-Mississippi—in between the lightning and the thunder—to see how many miles away the storm was.

They both looked around. "Wonder where it hit?"

John wouldn't be surprised to see a nearby tree split in two.

"We better get these clothes in the tent, batten down the hatches. Lightning that close, the rain's coming any minute."

"Agreed," John said.

Another FLASH! Then BOOM!!

Both men fell to the ground again.

"Lord Jesus," Alfred yelled out. "Save us, please."

Both men froze a few moments, then sat up.

"You okay?" Alfred asked.

"Yeah."

"Let's get inside the tent, right quick." Alfred hurried to the flap, zipped it open and disappeared inside.

John was right behind him. All the while, though, his fears only mounted. A tent offered no protection from a storm like this. Lightning could strike it—frying them inside—just as easy as it could strike any of the tall trees surrounding them. And a tent didn't lessen the frightening booms of thunder by a single decibel or the howling winds that sometimes came with these Florida storms. John had lost count how many times over the years he'd been hunkering down in a tent during a storm when it had simply blown right over, with him inside.

"Yes," John prayed silently, "Jesus, save us."

15

Over the next thirty minutes, John and Alfred sat huddled helplessly in the tent as the storm pounded the campsite. Neither one said very much. John could tell Alfred was just as scared by the look on his face, and by how much he drank. Right now, John missed that instant refuge. But he'd never return there so instead he toughed it out, tried not to let Alfred see how afraid he was.

Finally, the rain dropped to a steady drizzle and the booms of thunder grew further apart and less intense. It was then that John heard a new sound, this one occurring inside the tent. Alfred heard it, too. They both turned around and looked up.

"Shoot, thought I had that leak fixed." It was dripping pretty steady.

"Apparently not." John's eyes followed the direction of the drops. They ran off the middle seam and slid down a few inches toward his side of the tent before falling to the ground. "Oh, man." A decent sized puddle had already formed on the tent floor. "My blanket." He quickly lifted his spare blanket off the floor. It was soaking wet. Now he saw what was under it. The hardback book he'd been reading. "Look at that." He lifted it out of the puddle.

"I'm sorry, John. Got me some of that leak-sealing spray at the flea market a few weeks ago. Supposed to guarantee it'll fix any leak. Course, I had no way of testing it until it rained just now."

"Well, stuff happens. I can get the blanket to dry out. Might have to walk over to the laundromat though. Not enough time left in the day for it to dry up before tonight. But I'm afraid this book is ruined. Oh well, got it for a buck at a used bookstore."

"Can't you get another one?"

"It's over twenty years old. The guy said it's out of print." By now, it had stopped dripping. John set it down on an overturned crate that doubled as an end table. "Maybe it'll dry if we get a few good days of sun. Might be all warped but…don't worry about it. Can't be helped."

"Living the dream, right?" Alfred smiled, then laughed.

John noticed his eyes were glossed over. He said things like this when he'd graduated from a buzz to full-on drunk. And he'd always think the things he said were way funnier than they were.

John listened. It had stopped raining. But then another sound, something of a commotion. Voices, not too far away. Getting louder.

Alfred heard it, too. "Sounds like something's going on." He unzipped the flap, stuck his head out. "Bunch of folks rushing over toward the back end of the camp. "What's going on?" he asked a passerby.

"Lightning strike," the man said. "Folks are saying a big ole branch fell right on somebody's tent."

"Oh, no," Alfred said. "Anybody hurt?"

"Don't know. We're heading over there now to check it out." The fellow kept walking. Alfred pulled his head back inside and turned to John. "Who do we know lives over that way?"

"Doesn't Jenny? She's the only one I know that's over there."

A look of panic came over Alfred's face. "She does." He hurried out of the tent. "God, don't let it be her."

"You head out," John said. "I'm right behind you."

Minutes later, they were following a procession of camp inhabitants down a well-worn dirt path, all making their way to the same place. John and Alfred passed quite a few people along the way. John heard Alfred mumbling, "Lord, don't let it be her. Don't let it be her."

They turned a corner in the trail and John saw a small crowd forming up ahead. He also saw the tree that had grabbed everyone's attention, or what was left of it.

"Lord, would you look at that?" Alfred said.

The first and largest limb of a tall pine tree had cracked completely off. A thin strip along the bottom still clung to the trunk. The rest of it, the heaviest part, angled down toward the ground. There were too many people in the way to see where it actually landed. The way people acted, it seemed pretty obvious the limb had crushed someone's tent.

"Oh my gosh, John. That's where Jenny's tent is."

When they got nearer, both let out a sigh of relief. It wasn't Jenny's tent but the one right next to it. Through a gap in the crowd, they could see Jenny's tent plainly and her Christmas decorations all hanging where they were supposed to be.

As they reached the main group, everyone started backing up, responding to Hampton's commands.

"Is he all right?" someone asked.

"I'm afraid he's not. Poor Mr. Wilkins here is deceased."

Gasps and groans rose throughout the crowd. People stood in stunned disbelief. Some moved out of the way. John's curiosity got the better of him, and he looked down. The main part of the limb had come right down on the center of the tent, crushing it. He could see two legs peeking out from the opening by the flap in front.

"The poor thing," a woman said. "Did he suffer, or did it take him quick?"

"I'd say he didn't know what hit him," Hampton said. "You all heard how fast that lightning was hitting all around here. Just a flash, then the boom half a second later. I think that's how quick it was for him."

"Could've been anyone of us, the way that storm was acting," another man said.

"It certainly could," Hampton said. "Well listen, there's really nothing we can do here. Authorities are on the way. We should make sure they have a clear path back here, so they can do what they need to do."

"What he means is," Alfred whispered, "everybody scram. But before we go back toward our spot, I want to make sure Jenny's okay."

"I don't see her in this crowd," John said.

"Me neither. That's why I'm concerned."

"I'm sure she's fine."

"Maybe so. But I still want to make sure."

They weaved their way through the crowd, now mostly going in the opposite direction toward Jenny's tent. Alfred got close enough to call in after her, see if she was inside. But he stopped. He could hear a woman crying. "Jenny, is that you?"

The crying stopped. "It's me. That you, Alfred?"

"It is. Me and John out here. We're just checking in on you. Heard all that commotion going on here after the storm. We were afraid that limb had hit your tent."

"For a minute or two, I thought it had," Jenny said.

"So why you crying?" Alfred said. "Did you get hurt any?"

"No. I'm just very sad. I was starting to become friends with Mr. Wilkins. Talked to him at lunch today. He was finally starting to open up a little. I can't believe he's gone, just like that."

The two men were still standing outside her tent. "It's a terrible thing someone having to die like that." John said it to be comforting, but he wasn't sure he totally believed what he just said. In a way, he hoped when his time came, it might be something that quick. No chance to suffer, like some prolonged illness.

"You boys can come in if you want."

"Why thank you," Alfred said.

"I think I'm going to take a rain check on that. Sorry. Stupid thing to say. Anyway, my spare blanket got soaked from a hole in our tent. I gotta take it down to the laundromat. Want to get back before it gets dark."

"Or before another storm hits," Jenny said. "Supposed to be another one on its way."

Great, John thought. That's all he needed, another thunderstorm.

16

Jeffrey couldn't believe their Disney holiday trip was already over. By far, it was the best family vacation they had ever taken. Even with the crowds and long lines. They'd spent that first full day at Animal Kingdom, the next day at Disney Hollywood Studios, then Epcot, then they'd spent the final two days at the Magic Kingdom. Of course, Jeffrey thought the *FastPass* rides were the best. It was so much fun rushing past hundreds of people moving as slow as snails and getting right to the front of the line.

At the moment, they were each dragging their rolling suitcases down the long sidewalk toward the main lobby. The parking lot was just beyond that. Mom and Dad were moving quite a bit slower than they did on the way in. He'd heard them talking last night, after soaking in the hot tub for half an hour, about how much their legs were killing them. Mom said they absolutely had to put the gym back into their schedule.

"Hey sport, you in a hurry to get home?"

Jeffrey slowed his pace and turned to see Dad about twenty

feet behind. "No, not especially."

"Then why you walking so fast?"

"I'm not. This is how I always walk. You and mom are just going slow." They had just walked by the fenced in area around the hot tub. "You want Lisa and I to wait in the lobby a little while, so you and Mom can soak your legs one more time before we go?"

Dad laughed. "That's pretty good, wiseguy. You think that one up yourself?"

"Yeah, I did." He stopped walking a few moments to let Dad catch up.

"So what do you think you're going to miss about this place the most?"

They were walking past the food court. Jeffrey pointed to it. "I think the waffles in there shaped like Mickey Mouse. I'm going to miss not having those every morning for breakfast."

"No," Dad said. "By this place, I meant Disney World. You know, what are you going to miss most about being here?"

"I don't know. It was so much fun. Everything we did. The only hard part was having to leave Riley every night at the kennel." Riley usually slept every night on a rug at the foot of Jeffrey's bed. "I'll miss this place, but I won't miss not having him with us."

"He seemed pretty happy to me," Dad said. "Every time we visited."

"He did, when we'd get there. But he'd always be so sad when we'd leave."

"Well, I'm sure he's a lot happier getting to be in a place

like that, so close to us, than if we put him in a kennel back home."

"I know."

"We'll just get these suitcases loaded in the car and head right over there to pick Riley up for good." He opened the glass door to the lobby, first for Jeffrey then for the ladies.

Jeffrey couldn't wait.

Riley wasn't sure what, but something different was going on this morning. For several days in a row, Jeffrey and the father would come to take him out every morning for his first walk. Then they would stay with him for a while as he played with the other dogs in the fenced-in area. Then they would leave him again for the rest of the day, sometimes until the next day. Other times they would come back at night. It was so hard to know what to expect. Riley really missed all his old routines.

Just when he thought he might be getting used to a new one, things got changed again. A short while ago, he'd heard the main door open, the wonderful sound of a jingling leash, then footsteps coming down the aisle. But there was only one set this time, not three. And he could tell even before he saw her, that it was the worker's footsteps, not Jeffrey's or the father's.

She was a nice lady and treated him very well, but she wasn't Jeffrey or anyone else in the family. What did it mean? Why was she the one who'd taken him out for his morning walk? Were they coming back? They had to come back, didn't they?

They wouldn't leave him there for good.

He backed away off from the front of the gate, walked back to his bed and laid next to Monkey and Squirrel.

Had he been asleep for a few moments or a long while? Riley wasn't sure. Something nice had woken him up. The main door had opened. Several sets of footsteps were heading this way.

He froze a moment. He didn't hear it at first. But then, there it was. The jingling of the leash. Then an even better sound—Jeffrey's voice!

"Riley, we're here to get you, boy. Time to go home."

HOME? Did Riley just hear that word? He pressed his nose up against the door, trying to look down the aisle.

"There he is," Jeffrey said, excitedly. "I see him."

Riley loved the sound of his voice most of all, especially when it was happy. Putting that together with the word *home* could only be one thing. Riley started leaping up on the kennel door.

"Okay Riley, you need to calm down a little." It was the kennel worker. "I need you to back up, so I can get this door open, get this leash on you. You want to go home, right?"

Through his excitement, Riley connected with three of her words: *down, back* and *home*. He had to get control of himself. But how could he? Jeffrey and the father were standing right there. Finally, he stopped jumping and backed up, so she could come in.

"Good boy. Now sit…sit."

He did.

"Can I do his leash?" Jeffrey asked.

"Sure." She handed him the leash.

He stepped in as she backed out. Riley started jumping again. He couldn't help it. He was all over Jeffrey.

"You need to calm down, Riley, so I can put on your leash. Don't you want to go home?"

He didn't understand most of what Jeffrey said, but he definitely heard the word *home* again. That's all that mattered. They weren't going to leave him here. They did come back.

And now they were going home.

17

"Have you found out where we're at on the map yet?" Dad asked.

Jeffrey wasn't into this little exercise nearly as much as his father was. He'd rather be left alone to use his tablet for playing something fun, like a game. When he'd asked if they could not do this anymore on the drive down to Disney five days ago, Dad said it was part of his job to teach things like this to his kids. When Jeffrey had answered that he'd rather be playing a game, Dad had said they could turn this map project into a game.

Jeffrey wanted to say, but didn't, that this didn't qualify because games were usually fun. "Why can't you show Lisa how to do it?"

"Because he asked you, Jeffrey. Besides, I already know how."

Jeffrey sighed. "What am I supposed to be looking for again?"

"Where we're at right now."

"Can't we just look at the GPS to find that out?"

"What if the GPS is unavailable? Say you're in a car that doesn't have it? Or a big meteorite hits the satellites, and they don't work."

"Dad, if that happens we got bigger problems than just the GPS doesn't work. Google Maps wouldn't work, either. The whole internet would be down."

"Then you'd have to use an old-fashioned paper map. But how could you use it, if you didn't know how to read it?"

Jeffrey and Lisa looked at each other and rolled their eyes.

"Tom," Mom interjected, "do we even have a paper map in this car? I don't think we do."

"We probably don't, but that's not the point. If we needed one, we could get one. But what good would that do if Jeffrey didn't know how to read it? I'm trying to teach him a basic life lesson, one every guy should know."

"In case a big asteroid comes," Mom said, with a smirk.

"No, Mom," Lisa added. "He said a meteorite. A meteorite hits the satellite."

"Okay, a meteorite then."

Jeffrey enjoyed this back and forth.

"You guys go ahead and laugh," Dad said. "But it could happen."

"What about that Ice Age movie we saw?" Lisa said, "It showed a meteorite strike killed all the dinosaurs? Like Jeffrey said, seems like we'd have a lot more to worry about than losing our GPS."

Dad didn't answer. Jeffrey could tell, he wasn't having fun

anymore. He decided it was time to step in. "Okay, I'm looking at the map on my tablet. What am I supposed to be looking for?"

"We're about a hundred miles north of Disney World," Dad said. "Maybe a hundred and ten."

"What was the last town we passed?" Jeffrey said.

"The last bigg-ish town was Ocala. That's where we got off the big highway. Don't you remember I showed you the signs for 301 North? Can you find either one of those things on the map?"

Jeffrey looked until he found them. "Okay, I see 301."

"Now follow it north until you get to a place where there are no towns anywhere around. Cause that's where we are, out in the boondocks somewhere."

Jeffrey traced the road called 301 upwards with his eyes until he found a place with no cities nearby. Not even any small towns. He looked out the windows. Nothing but trees, trees and more trees. "All right, I think I know exactly where we're at. What do I do now?"

"Nothing. You don't do anything now. You just have the satisfaction of knowing where you are on the earth, and that you're not lost, and that you know how to find out where you're at by reading a map the old-fashioned way."

Jeffrey didn't know what to say. He didn't feel any satisfaction. Maybe it was one of those things he would feel later on when he got older.

The car hit a pothole and bounced up and down.

"Whoa," Dad said. "That'll do wonders for the alignment."

Riley's head popped up. He had been sound asleep for the last hour. He stood and stretched, yawned a couple of times. Then he started to get fidgety. He stepped over Jeffrey's legs and pressed his nose against the window.

"Dad, Riley just woke up. I think he has to go."

"He might just have to hold it for a little while. I don't think they have rest areas on small roads like this."

Jeffrey patted him and tried to get him to calm down. It wasn't working. "Dad, he's acting like he really has to go."

Lisa jumped in. "Can't we just pull over somewhere? He's a dog. He doesn't need a rest stop."

"No, but I do," Dad said.

"Well Tom, you might have to wait for the next gas station or convenience store. But Riley can go anywhere there's a little bit of grass." She pointed out the window. "There's grass everywhere you look between the road and the pine trees."

"All right, let me find a safe place to pull over. Jeffrey, you go ahead and hook up his leash."

"I never took it off," Jeffrey said. He could barely get Riley to stand still long enough to grab the leash handle. "He must really have to go." Riley stood on Jeffrey's legs trying to look out the window. Finally, Jeffrey was able to reach around him and get the leash.

"Okay," Dad said, "here's a nice long straight stretch of road. I'm going to pull over, Jeffrey. You got Riley ready?"

"All set."

"Pull way off the road, Tom," Mom said. "Don't want some texting driver to run into us from behind. There's plenty of grass here. You shouldn't get stuck."

Dad didn't answer her, but he did do what she asked. A few moments later, the car came to a stop.

"Are you going to go out with them?" Mom asked.

"I'm not gonna go out in the woods. I can wait till we stop somewhere."

"I'm not talking about you going to the bathroom. Just to make sure he feels safe. He's just a boy, Tom."

"I can do this myself," Jeffrey said. "It's just like walking him at home."

"Well, you go all the way over to the edge of the woods and walk him there."

"I will." Jeffrey opened the door.

"Hold on tight to that leash," Mom said.

"I will."

Dad opened his car door. "I'll stand out there with you. I'll just stay up here by the car."

"You don't have to."

"I know. But just go on. Don't worry about me. You'll be fine."

Riley leapt out of the car onto the grass ahead of Jeffrey. He quickly began straining at the end of the leash. Jeffrey let him lead the way. He headed straight for the woods, his head constantly moving back and forth as he sniffed the grass.

He startled to angle to the right as they got closer to the tree line. It was like he was on a mission, like he'd picked up the scent of something. Jeffrey pulled back on the leash, trying to get his attention. "Riley, c'mon. It's time to hurry up." *Hurry up* was the phrase they'd always used since he was a puppy when they'd take him for bathroom walks. But Riley just kept straining at the end of the leash, following this scent.

When they reached the woods, the call of nature must have overcome his curiosity, because he suddenly stopped pulling and lifted his leg on a tree. He held that pose for the longest time.

Suddenly, his head shot straight forward, looking down the tree line. His body stiffened and his ears perked up.

Everything happened so fast.

Jeffrey looked down the line to see what had caught Riley's attention. A rabbit had jumped into the clearing about thirty yards away. It saw them, turned and stood on its hind legs. Riley let loose that screaming-bark of his. In a flash, he tore off after it. The rabbit disappeared into the thick brush. Jeffrey tightened his grip on the leash and braced himself for the moment Riley reached the end.

Then something crazy happened.

When Riley got to the end of the leash, there was only the briefest pause, then something happened—Riley kept running after the rabbit. He was no longer on the leash! It had broken.

"Riley!" he screamed. He started running after him, as fast as he could. "Riley, come back!"

He couldn't catch him. He was too fast. In a moment, Riley disappeared into the woods in the same spot where the rabbit had gone. "Riley, stop!"

"Jeffrey, wait! What are you doing? Where are you going? Stop." Dad shouted from the car. But Jeffrey couldn't stop.

"Riley!" he yelled.

18

Riley couldn't believe his eyes. The rabbit he was chasing was real, not a toy. When he first saw it there in the grass, he thought it had to be. But then it moved. Toys don't move. Not unless he was playing fetch and Jeffrey threw it. But this rabbit moved. It looked right at Riley. It stood up then darted into the woods.

How could he *not* chase after it?

As he neared the spot where it ran into the trees, Riley was suddenly aware of two things: first, he was no longer attached to the leash and, second, the rabbit actually had a scent. In this thick underbrush, that was so important if he was gonna catch this thing. And he *would* catch it. He had to.

When would he ever get a chance like this again?

For the first fifty yards or so, the rabbit seemed to be following a narrow trail. He'd lost sight of it seconds after the chase began, but the scent was very strong. Suddenly, the scent took a sharp left. Riley had to close his eyes as leaves and branches began slapping him in the face. Moments later, the scent took a right turn. The rabbit had picked up a new path. He could open his eyes again.

All the while, he barked and screamed for all he was worth. He wasn't sure why, but he couldn't help it. This went on for several minutes. The rabbit zigzagged deeper into the woods with Riley hot on his trail. By the strength of the scent he could tell that, several times, he had gained on the critter, only to lose ground when the rabbit made a sharp turn one way or the other. Riley couldn't turn as fast as the rabbit.

Finally, about fifteen minutes into the chase, and just about the time Riley could feel his energy level was almost spent, the rabbit got back on another trail. This one was long and straight and easy to see. Riley made a mad dash forward, giving it everything he had.

The rabbit's scent grew stronger and stronger. Then he saw it! Just up ahead, the fluffy white tail bobbing up and down as it ran. He was so close. Just a few more minutes, and he'd have it in his mouth.

He was no longer just running, he was leaping great strides, throwing his front feet forward, hoping to grab a few extra inches every time. He was closing the gap. It was now only a matter of seconds.

Then suddenly…it was gone. The rabbit disappeared. How was that possible? It was there one moment, then it wasn't. Where did it go? It happened near the base of a large oak tree. Huge roots protruded from the ground in every direction. He ran around the tree once, twice, a third time. The rabbit was nowhere to be found. But its scent still hung so strong in the air. He continued tracing it, moving a little slower in case he had missed something.

He backtracked his own footsteps up the trail about fifteen yards, just to make sure the scent hadn't turned left or right before the tree roots appeared. No, that wasn't the problem. Tracing the scent back again brought him to the exact same place.

Then he noticed something he hadn't seen before. Under the biggest root there was a small hole that seemed to disappear under the tree. He stuck his nose in it. Yes, the scent was so strong right here. But how was that possible? He could barely get his nose three inches into it; how could a rabbit fit its whole body in there?

With his nose fixed to the ground, he walked slowly around the tree looking for some trace of the scent leaving the tree in a different direction. After the third time around, he found it. It wasn't nearly as strong as the scent at the entrance of the hole, but it was definitely the same scent. The rabbit must have come out on this side and continued running away from him.

Riley followed the scent as it moved away from the tree, deeper into the woods. He couldn't let this rabbit get away. When would he ever get the chance to chase a real rabbit again?

"Riley! Riley, come back!"

Jeffrey kept running further and further into the woods. He couldn't see Riley anymore, though he could still faintly hear his high-pitched squealing bark. Branches and palm fronds slapped into him, slowing his progress. He felt the sting each time one hit his shins, neck and face. He ignored the pain and kept running. "Riley. Stop! Come back!"

"Jeffrey, stop!" It was his dad.

"I can't, Dad. I'll lose him."

"You have to, it's too dangerous in there."

Jeffrey kept running, pretending he didn't hear. Suddenly, his right foot sank below the ground. He tried to pull it out, but his momentum kept the rest of his body moving forward. His ankle twisted and he fell flat on his face, bruising his knee on something hard. Searing pain shot up through his leg, and he screamed.

"Jeffrey!"

"My leg!"

"I can't see you."

"I'm here. Dad, it hurts so much." He didn't want to cry, but he did. The pain was just too much. He tried to lift his foot out of the hole. The pain. He couldn't do it. "Dad!"

He lifted both arms in the air, hoping Dad could see them. Finally, a terribly long minute later he heard the sound of footsteps rushing through the woods nearby. "Jeffrey?"

"I'm right here." He began waving his arms back and forth.

"I see you."

Dad's blurry face appeared above him. He wiped the tears away. Dad's eyes shifted down toward his foot, and he made a face.

"It's already swelling," Dad said. "I hope it's not broken."

"Can you see Riley?"

Dad looked up, his head swiveled back and forth scanning the trees and the ground. "No, sorry. I don't see him. But I can't worry about him now. We've got to get you to an emergency room, get that foot looked at."

Jeffrey stopped crying. "But Dad, what about Riley? We can't leave him out here in the woods by himself. Remember the map? We were looking at it a little while ago. There aren't even any towns nearby. He can't survive in the woods."

"I'm sorry, Jeffrey. I don't know what to tell you, son. There's nothing I can do about it. He's nowhere in sight. And these woods are no place for us to be roaming around in, even if you could walk, which you can't. I was trying to get you to stop because of things like bears and rattlesnakes. Didn't even think about you getting hurt like this. But that foot has to be looked at. I don't even know how far we'll have to drive to see a doctor. But we have to get you back in the car and leave right now. We'll just have to pray and ask God to keep Riley safe."

Jeffrey started to cry again. Much harder than a minute ago. "Dad, we can't just leave him. He'll be all alone."

"I'm so sorry, son." Dad bent over and lifted him off the ground.

A new wave of pain shot up through Jeffrey's leg. But the pain in his heart hurt so much worse than his ankle.

19

Jeffrey's father carried him in his arms back through the woods toward the highway. They reached the grassy area and were now almost at the car.

"Tom, what happened? Jeffrey, are you all right?" His mom rushed toward them.

"Jeffrey fell while he was running and twisted his ankle. I don't know if it's broken or just sprained, but it's definitely starting to swell up."

"We gotta get him to an emergency room," she said.

"I know. Could you get on Google maps, find out where the nearest one is?"

"Where's Riley?" Lisa asked.

Hearing that, Jeffrey started crying again.

"He's still in the woods?" she said.

"Yes," Dad said. "He took off after a rabbit. I have no idea where he is. He ran off so far we couldn't even hear him barking anymore. Can you open Jeffrey's car door?"

Lisa did, then got out of the way.

"Jeffrey, I'm going to put you down on your seat. But you can't sit the normal way with your foot down on the floor."

"Right," Mom said, "you need to prop that ankle up."

"So I want you to sit sideways with your hurt leg propped up across the seat."

"Get one of the bed pillows from the back," Mom said. "It needs to be a little higher than straight."

"Then where am I going to sit?" Lisa said.

"Where you always sit," Dad said. But you're going to have to let Jeffrey rest his foot on your lap. The seat's just not wide enough. Lisa, can you grab that pillow?" He laid Jeffrey down in the back seat.

"Oww!" Pain shot up his leg when it bumped the front seat.

"I'm sorry. I'm trying to be as gentle as I can."

Dad took the pillow from Lisa. "You get in, so I can lay this across your lap." He looked at Jeffrey. I'm going to need to lift your legs, just for a moment, so Lisa can get in the car. It might hurt a little."

It didn't hurt a little. It hurt a lot. But Jeffrey tried not to let it show.

Lisa got in. Dad set the pillow down on her lap and gently lowered Jeffrey's bad ankle. Jeffrey winced but suppressed the urge to cry.

"Okay," Mom said, "I found the nearest ER. It's about eighteen minutes from here. A little town called Summerville, right up the road."

"Great. We'll head there right now."

"But Dad," Lisa said. "What about Riley?"

Jeffrey was surprised to hear her speak up. "Please Dad, can't we wait here a little while. Maybe he'll come back."

"And maybe he won't," Dad said. "The few times he's gotten out at home he didn't come back on his own. Remember? We had to get in the car and drive all over until we found him. I'm really sorry about Riley, guys. Really, I am. But we can't sit here and wait for him. Look at your ankle, Jeffrey. It's even bigger now than when I found you in the woods."

Jeffrey did look at his ankle. He had never been hurt like this before. It looked like his foot had swallowed a softball. It hurt like crazy, and now it was starting to throb.

Dad started the car, checked to make sure the road was clear and drove off. Jeffrey glanced back through the rear window, staring at the place where Riley had disappeared into the woods, hoping to see him somehow reappear again. He continued staring at that spot until the car turned left on a sharp curve, and a new section of trees blocked it from view.

He turned around and looked out the side window. Images of Riley began to parade through his mind, followed by a new surge of tears.

Riley finally reached a place where he had to admit defeat. It wasn't that he could no longer smell any trace of the rabbit, it was that so many other conflicting smells had gotten in the way. This section of the woods was full of them, going in a variety of different directions.

He stopped running, sniffed the air a few more times, then turned around and started heading back. It was time to find Jeffrey. He let out one of his loudest barks, then listened. There was no reply, so he tried it several more times. Still, no response. He put his nose close to the ground and searched for his own scent. It took a few minutes to isolate it but, when he did, it became fairly easy to retrace his steps back through the woods toward the road.

Along the way, he barked loudly several times calling out to get Jeffrey's attention. Each bark was met with silence. Finally, he reached the edge of the woods, broke through it, and now stood in the grass. But something was wrong. Jeffrey was nowhere in sight. Neither were the other members of the family.

He was certain this was the place. But where were they? Where was the car? He smelled the grass again. There was Jeffrey's scent, right where it was supposed to be. The father's also. He began to follow back through the grass as it angled toward the road. Just as he got to the place where the scent stopped, a car raced by on the road, beeping its horn. It frightened him, and he ran back to the edge of the woods.

He didn't understand why they would leave him. What was he supposed to do? Should he wait there for them until they came back?

20

The pain was almost unbearable. Jeffrey tried playing a game on his tablet, but the spasms were too distracting. As soon as they'd reached the outskirts of this town, they pulled into a convenience store to get some ice. Mom's idea. She thought it might ease the pain. It didn't make any difference at first, but now, fifteen minutes later, it did seem to be helping a little.

"Almost there, Jeffrey," Mom said. She reached her hand back behind the seat.

He grabbed hold of it and squeezed gently. "How many more minutes do you think?"

"Less than five," Dad said.

"After we're done at the hospital, can we go back to where we last saw Riley and see if he's come out of the woods?"

"Maybe. Let's wait and see what happens here. But I tell you what I will do...as soon as you're situated in the ER, I'll call the Highway Patrol and tell them what happened. Maybe they can send a car to drive up and down that part of 301 and keep their eye out for Riley. Since he's black and white, he should be pretty easy to spot if he's anywhere near the road."

"But couldn't we do it too?"

"Maybe we can. Let's wait and see. Did he have his collar on with his name tag?"

"I think so."

"Don't be so sure of that," Lisa said. "Maybe it broke off when he pulled away from you." She bent down and picked up something from the floor of the car. As she did, she bumped his foot.

"Owww!"

"I'm sorry." She quickly straightened back up. "Here's what's left of it."

Jeffrey looked. She was holding the leash. It was clipped to a thin, oddly shaped piece of metal wire. He wasn't sure what he was seeing. "What is that?"

"Jeffrey, what did you hook his leash up to back at the kennel," Lisa said.

"The ring on his collar. Where I always do."

"Looks like you didn't this time," she said. "Know what I think you did? This looks like the little ring that held his name tag to the collar. You thought you clicked it on the right ring, but I think you hung it on the name tag ring by mistake. So when he pulled so hard like that going after the rabbit, it just bent right off."

"Oh, no." As he looked at what she held in her hands, it made perfect sense. "That means it's all my fault. Riley's lost because of me. No one will know who he is without his name tag." He started crying again.

"That's okay, Jeffrey," Mom said. "Don't be so hard on yourself. It was an accident. Let's just pray God will keep him safe until we, or someone else finds him."

No one said anything for a few moments.

"He looks very distinctive with his black and white spots," Mom said, "and he comes to his name when you call him. That should be enough for a policeman, if they actually see him. Don't you think?"

"You're probably right," Dad said.

"Okay, there's the hospital," Mom said, "See the sign up there on the right?"

"I do."

Jeffrey looked, expecting a tall building to come into view. But when they got there, that's not what it was.

"That's a pretty small hospital," Dad said.

"Summerville's a pretty small town," Mom replied. "But I think they can handle a twisted ankle."

He pulled into the parking area following the signs to the ER. "Okay, Jeffrey. I'm going to carry you inside until we find a wheelchair. It might hurt a little getting you out of the car."

Riley continued to hang around the area where he had last seen the car. But he'd moved further back near the edge of the woods after several cars raced by and scared him. He was so confused. He didn't know where Jeffrey or the family had gone, or when they were coming back.

So far, and for as long as he could remember, they always

came back. No matter where they'd left him. But this felt different. He couldn't read this situation at all.

He laid down to rest a few minutes and soon became aware of how thirsty he was. Where would he get a drink? He always drank out of a bowl. Humans always provided his water in a bowl. At home, it was mostly Jeffrey. Sometimes the mother. Even at the place he'd just left, for several days someone had always provided him a fresh bowl of water. He hadn't seen a bowl anywhere around here.

As he laid there pondering this, he remembered when he was deep in the woods he'd run across a place that had puddles. He stood, took a few steps toward the road but stopped. Two cars came flying by going in opposite directions. Neither one was the family car.

He decided to head back into the woods and trace the original trail he'd followed earlier when chasing that rabbit. Once he found the puddles, he would sniff around some more, see if he could find fresh water.

Maybe by the time he did this and came back, the family car would be here again.

21

Jeffrey sat in a hospital bed in the Summerville hospital's ER. He had just come back from having x-rays taken of his foot. It was propped up on a pillow with an ice bag over it. They had given him something for the pain, so it didn't hurt as bad as before.

"Can we leave pretty soon and go back and look for Riley?"

"We have to wait here till we find out what they're going to do," Mom said. "If your foot's broken, they might have to set it."

"What does that mean?"

"It doesn't hurt. They would put you to sleep first, then fix it up while you're out. You'd wake up and your foot will be in a cast."

"I've had a broken ankle before," Dad said. "When I was a few years older than you. Hurt it playing football. And your mom's right, it doesn't hurt a bit."

"But how long will that take?" Jeffrey asked.

"I don't know," Mom said. We'll just have to wait."

A few minutes later, the doctor walked in. "Well, your foot's not broken. That's the good news. The bad news is, you sprained it pretty badly. Sometimes a bad sprain can take longer to heal than a fracture. But we won't need to set it, so you'll be able to leave here in an hour or two. After we wrap it up and get you some crutches."

"I'll be on crutches? For how long? Till Christmas?"

The doctor nodded yes. "Possibly for several weeks after Christmas, depending on how well it heals." He looked at Jeffrey's parents. "You should check in with his regular doctor when you get back home. He'll advise you about the progress and let you know when Jeffrey can come off the crutches. The nurse will give you a document that will probably answer most of your questions about how to care for him at home."

Mom and Dad thanked him. He shook hands with them and left.

"Well, I think what I'm going to do," Dad said, "is make better use of my time. The doc said Jeffrey was gonna be here for another hour or two. Instead of me sitting around here doing nothing, I could drive back to where we lost Riley, see if I can find him. I could be there and back way before we're done here."

"Are you okay if Daddy leaves?" Mom asked Jeffrey.

"To find Riley? Yes. I just wish I could come too."

"Great." Dad reached down and gave the toes on Jeffrey's good foot a gentle squeeze. "I'll be back before you know it. Hopefully, with Riley."

"Tom," Mom said. "I'll walk out with you."

Tom was pretty sure he knew what his wife wanted to talk about. He tensed up as she approached him in the hall.

"Before we left for Disney, did you follow through on that thing? You know, going online to update Riley's chip info on that website?"

Tom swallowed hard and looked down at the ground.

"You didn't?"

He looked back at her and shook his head no. The look on her face, anger mixed with disappointment, filled him with regret. "We were rushing around so much, I...I completely forgot."

"So even if anyone finds Riley, there's no guarantee they'll connect him with us."

"I'm sorry. I screwed up. I'll call them now. Maybe we can take care of it over the phone. I mean, if someone finds Riley, it will still take some time before they get him someplace that has the ability to scan his chip, right? If I get it updated now, it still might not be too late."

She glared at him. "I hope you're right. I can't believe you never called."

"I'm sorry."

She sighed. "I hope you find him." She walked back into the room where Jeffrey was.

Tom walked down the hallway toward the parking lot. He stopped briefly at a waiting area and took out his phone. He looked up the non-emergency number for the Florida Highway Patrol.

"Florida Highway Patrol, how can I direct your call?"

"Hi, my name's Tom Mitchell. I'm calling from the ER in a little town called Summerville. I'm wondering if you guys can do us a favor. It's not really an emergency. Well, it kind of is for our family. But no one is in danger."

"How can I help you, sir?"

"About an hour ago, we were driving north on 301, about fifteen miles south of where I am now. It's a real wooded area. No homes or businesses nearby for several miles. Anyway, our dog had to go to the bathroom, so we pulled well off the side of the road, and my son walked him on a leash in a grassy area close to the tree line. I guess he saw some kind of small animal and took off after it."

"So, he broke free from the leash?" the dispatcher said.

"Yeah. Looks like my son clipped the leash to his dog tag instead of the metal ring on his collar, and it broke when the dog got to the end of it. His name's Riley, by the way."

"Well sir, I'm very sorry your dog got away, but the Highway Patrol doesn't do searches for lost pets. To be honest with you, I'm not sure any of the Animal Control Officers in any of the nearby towns could help you out with this, either. The area you described is well out of their jurisdiction."

"Yeah, I figured that. I'm just wondering if I gave you the description of our dog, if any of your officers were driving along 301 and they spotted him, they could stop the car and call out to him. Riley loves people, and I'm sure considering how scared he must be, he'd come right to anyone who called him in a pleasant voice."

There was a long pause. Finally, the woman said, "I'll take

down your information but will have to talk to my supervisor to see if he's okay with what you're asking. We can't take any chances that a dog might bite our officers. They don't have the kind of dog-catching equipment an Animal Control Officer would have."

"I understand," Tom said. "But I'd appreciate it if you'd ask. Seriously, Riley would never bite anyone. He'd probably come running and jump into their arms and start licking them all over."

The dispatcher laughed. "Well, I will pass on what you've asked and include what you said about your dog's temperament."

"Thank you very much. That's all I can ask."

"You have a good day, and I hope you find your dog."

Tom decided to take a seat to make it easier to go online, so he could interact with the pet website that controlled Riley's chip information. He couldn't figure out exactly what to do on the website and didn't want to take a chance that he'd mess this up, so he got on their Contact Page and hammered out a detailed message, explaining the situation. Hopefully someone would email him or call him back soon.

He put his phone back in his pocket and headed down the doorway to the ER parking lot.

About twenty minutes later, Tom arrived at the area where he believed they had lost Riley. But it was just a guess. He wished he had marked the spot on his GPS before they'd left for the hospital, but in all the excitement he'd forgotten to do it. Sadly, there were no distinguishing features to the scenery outside. The entire area was flat and covered on both sides of the road with pine trees, pine trees and more pine trees.

When he had pulled over before, he'd looked for a long straight section of road. The problem was, that described about half the roadways out here. The other half were curvy sections going one way or the other.

The best he could do was drive by some of the straight sections as slowly as safely possible and hope Riley would be out in the open somewhere, or at least not very deep in the woods. His bright white and dark spots should stand out like a sore thumb.

He checked his rearview mirror to make sure he was alone on the road, then slowed down to just under 50mph. Driving along, he scanned the left side of the road, hoping against hope to see him.

But in his heart, he knew this task was really more about being able to tell his son that they had done everything they could before heading back home to Savannah.

22

Kim Harper made one last walk-through the kennel, just to make sure things were ready. Taylor Saunders had surprised her, responding quickly to an email invitation she'd sent yesterday to come check out some of the dogs she'd selected for his new project, Dignity Pond.

He was on his way to the shelter now.

She didn't know why she was so nervous. Their last and only visit together had been quite pleasant. He was surprisingly normal and easy to talk to. It probably didn't help that after they'd left the Sierra House restaurant, she went back to her apartment and began checking him out on the internet. Maybe it was the pictures of him standing beside the airliner or the helicopter with his name emblazoned across the fuselage. Maybe it was the entire page full of luxury subdivisions and estate homes he'd developed from scratch, all with matching PGA golf courses. Or the skyscraper-condominiums he'd built in Miami, Tampa and Jacksonville. Or that he was half-owner of a NASCAR racing team.

She had never been with a millionaire before, let alone a billionaire. She trained dogs and had no ambitions of being anything else. She drove a nine-year-old car. Her 401(k) had just passed the fifty thousand mark.

A dog barked loudly in an effort to get her attention. It worked. She was standing right in front of her kennel. It was Kenzie, a beautiful mostly-yellow lab pup, about eight months old. Kim looked down and saw her sitting as close to the kennel door as possible, her eyes fixed on Kim's, her tail thumping up and down. "What, am I not paying attention to you? Standing here all this time without saying hi?" She bent down and pushed her three middle fingers through an opening in the kennel, stroking Kenzie's head. Kenzie quickly shifted so that she could lick Kim's fingers instead.

"You sweet girl. I wish I could take you out right now. But I will very soon." She was one of the dogs Kim had earmarked for Taylor's program. She glanced at the clock on the wall. It was time to head out to the lobby and meet him. He seemed like a pretty punctual guy. "I'll be back to see you in a few minutes."

She walked down the aisle and through the doorway into the hallway that led to the lobby area.

As she stepped into the lobby, a shiny black Jaguar drove by the front glass doors.

"I think Mr. Right just arrived," Anne said, sitting at the receptionist desk. She looked back toward Kim. "You're not wearing your evening gown."

"Oh, stop. He's not here to see me."

"Then I have a chance?"

Kim laughed. "He's here to look at some of the dogs I selected for his new housing project."

"That new homeless village you were telling me about?"

"That's the one." Kim walked up to the front door and looked left out the window, trying to get a glimpse of his car as it pulled into an open slot. "Very nice." Did she just say that out loud?

"I know, right?" Anne said.

"I was talking about the car."

"That, too. They're both nice."

"Now stop, he's coming this way." Kim backed up several paces.

"Good," Anne said, "don't want to give the impression that you're crazy about him. Men like it better when you play hard to get."

Kim sighed loudly.

He was coming up the front sidewalk now. He looked through the glass, saw her and smiled. She thought about opening the door for him but remembered what Anne had just said about appearing overly anxious.

He came in and said, "There you are, Kim. So good to see you again." He reached out his hand.

"Great to see you, too." She turned toward Anne. "I don't know if you remember—"

"—Anne, right? You were here last time."

"I was. Can't believe you remembered my name."

"One of my aunts is named Anne. She even has red hair like you."

"How nice," Anne said. "She must be a wonderful person."

Taylor laughed. "She is. Well, anyway...nice to see you again, Anne." He turned to Kim. "So, you have some dogs to show me?"

"I do." They started walking toward the kennels. Kim glanced back at Anne, who gave her a wink and a thumb's up. "Did you get that file I sent you yesterday, the one that lays out the basic ideas I have in mind?"

"I did. Read it on my plane ride home last evening."

"That's right. You were taking a trip to the UK."

"Actually, that trip was only for two days. I was flying back from Toronto last night. Looks like they'll be getting a white Christmas this year." He opened the hallway door for her.

"I don't how you do it. Travel all over the place like that. Doesn't it mess up your sleep?"

"Sometimes. But I don't really like to travel that much anymore. Some of it can't be avoided, but whenever possible I use the internet and video-conferencing. I like that much better. It's probably cut down on half of my trips from a few years ago."

They arrived at the kennel door. "Before we go in," Kim said, "let me explain a few things. So far, I've put a hold on six dogs. I know you're hoping for a dozen, and we might still be able to reach that number the day after New Year's Day. That's when you open the doors at the village, correct?"

"That's our soft opening. The grand opening will be a week later."

"That might be a more realistic goal to get twelve dogs

ready. Most months this wouldn't be a hard task, but a lot of people like to get dogs for Christmas presents. So we have a lot of them moving through the shelter, especially the last half of December."

"Do many of them get turned back in a month later?"

"They tell me before I came it was quite a high percentage, usually within the first two months. Which is really a heartbreaking thing for the dog. People have no idea the level of emotion dogs go through. But we've brought that return rate way down by offering group training classes in January to people who adopt dogs for Christmas presents as part of the package. The truth is, maybe ninety percent of the reasons people bring their dogs back can be easily fixed through training. So by offering it right when they adopt the dog, we nip that problem in the bud."

"That's…pretty cool. I imagine it has to be pretty satisfying for you, being able to make that kind of a difference."

"It really is. Nothing makes me happier than seeing a dog and their owner really bonding and connecting well together."

"Nothing?"

"Well, nothing from a work standpoint, I mean." She thought about it a moment, but decided not to say it. Since she didn't have much of a private life to speak of lately, the satisfaction she felt from working with dogs *was* probably the high point of her life on any given day.

"So tell me more about the dogs you picked out for me. I mean, for the village."

"I pretty much followed the same protocols I'm using for

selecting the prison pups. Since those dogs wind up with veterans wrestling with PTSD, I'm thinking their emotional needs are probably similar to people who've been dealing with homelessness for many years. One big difference is the fact that your dogs won't be bonding with just one person, like the prison pups do. Since they'll be interacting with more than one owner, I've spent more time making sure the dogs on our list are extremely good with people."

"Like someone who's a 'people-person' you're looking for a people-dog?" Taylor said.

"Yes. That's the biggest thing. They'll still be smart dogs who respond well to training, but I'm really going for people factor." She opened the door, and they walked into the kennel. "The first dog I want to introduce you to might be my favorite of the whole group. She's the kind of dog that makes my job a lot harder, because every time I'm with her I have to resist the urge to adopt her myself."

She walked over to the first kennel on the right. "Taylor, meet Kenzie. Kenzie, meet Taylor."

23

Tom was sad as he pulled into the hospital parking lot. He'd been driving back and forth on Highway 301 in the general area where Riley had gone missing for as long as he could. During the drive, he'd called his wife and asked her to text him when Jeffrey was about twenty minutes from being released to go home. When that text had finally come, Tom had to fight back tears as he drove away.

Riley had been such a great dog for their family. It would've been hard to stop searching for him if he'd been lost in a neighborhood. At least there they'd have the hope he'd soon be picked up by someone and properly taken care of. Even more likely be returned home within a day or two.

Here, Tom couldn't even be sure Riley would be safe, let alone ever be found. The area was so remote, miles away from the nearest town. Riley wouldn't know how to find food. Would he even find any fresh water to drink? Then a worse thought…Riley could become prey to some wild animal. He wasn't a big dog. If attacked, Tom wasn't even sure he'd know how to defend himself. He could cross paths with a bear or be bitten by a venomous snake. Although rare, there were even some panthers still running loose in certain parts of Florida. If only Tom had checked the leash back at the kennel or else walked Riley himself.

He turned the car off, dreading what he'd face in the next ten minutes. Whatever would he say to his son?

Riley lapped up the fresh water flowing from a creek he'd finally found a few minutes ago. But his ears remained on high alert. He stopped to look around at every unfamiliar sound. The truth was, almost every sound in these woods was unfamiliar.

Just as he finished drinking, he heard a totally new sound. He stopped, lifted his head then cocked it to hone in better. It was downwind and downstream from him. Sounded like water moving, but in small amounts, different from the sounds coming from the creek. He looked around. He couldn't see anything or smell anything unusual.

Suddenly, it stopped.

Another sound. Crunching leaves, twigs breaking. Small footsteps. He had an idea now where the new sounds were coming from. Had to be a creature, some kind of small animal. Was it the rabbit? If Riley had been in his backyard, he would've already taken off and closed in on it by now. But he was afraid. He didn't want to commit himself until a he knew what it was.

He began stepping lightly in the general direction of the sound. It stopped, so he stopped. All was quiet. Several moments ticked by. He began moving forward again, picking his steps carefully. A dragonfly zipped past his head, momentarily distracting him. He resisted the urge to chase it, but his next step came down on a pile of dry leaves. A loud crunch.

Something moved up ahead. He looked. A raccoon stood, saw him and squealed. It took off, jumped across the stream into the brush on the other side. Riley was hot on its tail. He leaped across the creek and easily picked up the scent.

The chase was on. It was so exciting.

Riley didn't know if he could catch it and, even if he did, what he would do with it. The main thing was not to lose it, like he'd lost the rabbit. They kept running deeper and deeper into the woods. The raccoon zigzagged as it ran, like the rabbit but in a much wider pattern. It didn't matter, it gave off a much stronger scent.

At one point, Riley could see it's back just up ahead. It turned right into some thick ferns. He was getting close.

Suddenly, it leapt from the ground onto a nearby tree and scampered up the trunk almost as fast as it ran on the ground. Riley leapt as high as he could but didn't even come close to catching it. For the next several minutes he ran around the tree, leaping and barking, demanding the raccoon come down. Of course, it wouldn't listen. He didn't really think it would. It was fun being in charge of the situation, just the same.

He stood back a few moments gazing up at the upper limbs.

The raccoon sat close to the main trunk, staring down at him. Their eyes locked for a moment. If it was trying to communicate something to him, Riley had no idea what it was. He had started feeling hungry a short while ago, but he never thought about eating the raccoon. If anything, he might want to play with it, maybe chase it around some more.

After walking around the tree and barking triumphantly a few more times, Riley began to feel tired. He lay down on a soft bed of leaves, deciding to just guard his prize for a while.

Before much time had passed, Riley fell fast asleep.

Riley was awakened by something that had interrupted his dreams, a deep rumbling sound that didn't fit. He was startled by what he saw when his eyes first opened. He'd forgotten that he'd fallen asleep all alone in the woods. The rumbling sound had disappeared, but he noticed something else…looking up, the sky through the trees had turned dark gray. He also noticed that the raccoon had disappeared. He must've climbed down and snuck off while Riley slept.

He stood and stretched and began to feel a tinge of fear. It took him a moment to understand why. It wasn't just that he was alone and had no idea where his family was, it was the dark sky overhead and what it meant. As if sending a signal to confirm his fears, that deep rumbling sound returned. Louder than in his dreams. Jeffrey called it "thunder." Riley hated thunder and the bright flashes of light that came with it.

At home, sometimes it got so loud it felt like the house was about to come crashing down on top of him. He would run to Jeffrey, who'd hold him until it was all done. If Jeffrey wasn't home, he would hide under Jeffrey's bed.

There! There it was again! And again, louder than before. It was getting closer. Half the sky was getting darker. His head whipped around in every direction, but where could he run and hide? He thought about that little hole the rabbit had disappeared into under that big tree root, wishing he could find a bigger hole just like that.

Since he couldn't recall a safe hideout in any of the places he had been to so far, he decided to go deeper into the woods, away from the approaching thunder. As he ran, he kept looking in every direction for something, anything, that would provide some protection for what was coming his way.

Just about the time he needed to stop and catch his breath, something off to the right caught his attention. A dark area in the midst of a cluster of trees. When he got closer, he saw two large trees had fallen over, one on top of the other. A layer of vines had grown up around them. The dark spot was located just below where the two trees met. Riley slowed, then stopped to check it out. He didn't smell anything in the air that concerned him.

BOOM!

A loud clap of thunder struck, so close it seemed to smack the ground right behind him. He leapt through the vines toward the dark spot, grateful to find it empty. He backed into it as far as he could and curled into a tight ball.

A moment later, the rains came in a fierce downpour. The

first few minutes he remained dry, then drops of water began to fall from several spots above his head. He didn't care.

At least in here, the thunder couldn't get him.

24

Jeffrey and his family arrived back at their home in Savannah around ten-thirty that night. His mom had to shake his shoulder several times to wake him in the backseat. He'd slept the whole way, probably because of the pain killers his mom had said. He was glad he'd stayed asleep, otherwise he would've cried the whole time. That's the first thing he did when he managed to make his way through the front doors on his new crutches.

Losing Riley was by far the worst thing he'd ever experienced. He felt lost inside. Mom held him on the couch and just let him cry for the next twenty minutes, while Dad and Lisa unloaded the car.

Hardly anyone said a word.

When Jeffrey stopped crying, Mom said, "It's time for your pain medicine again. It'll probably make you sleepy, again, but that's fine because it's really bedtime anyway. Rest is probably the thing you need most right now."

"How am I gonna get up the stairs with these?" He pointed at the crutches.

"Tonight, your dad's gonna carry you. I don't want you trying to go up or down the stairs on those things. You'll break your neck."

"I'm supposed to live downstairs now? The doctor said I'd be on them for a few weeks, maybe more."

"No, you're not going to live downstairs, but you definitely have to stay down here most of the time, except maybe at night for sleeping. Don't worry about that now. We'll figure out how we're going to handle this a little at a time. When you wake up tomorrow morning, call me or Dad. One of us will help you get out of bed."

"Okay. Are you going somewhere now?"

"I have to, Hon. I need to help Dad put some things away, so he can come and take you upstairs. Want me to turn the TV on? Might help you take your mind off things."

"Sure. I still feel pretty groggy, though."

"If you start to fall asleep, just let it happen. Dad can still carry you upstairs whether you're asleep or awake. You want the Disney channel or Nickelodeon?"

"I don't really care. Disney, I guess, since we were just there." Although, all the joy and fun that had piled up through the week seemed completely out of reach now.

She picked up the remote, turned the TV on and found the Disney channel. "You just watch this and, like I said, if you fall asleep, that's fine." She set it down on top of the TV stand and went into the kitchen.

To see the TV better, Jeffrey repositioned himself on the couch. As he did, he accidentally moved his ankle and felt a sharp pain. "Mom?" he yelled.

She came rushing out from the kitchen. "What's the matter?"

"Didn't you say it was time for my pain medicine?"

"You're right. I completely forgot. I'll be right back."

She returned with the pills and a small glass of milk. After he took the pills, she said, "Want me to leave the rest of the milk?"

"No thank you."

She left and he shifted his focus to the TV show. Looked like an episode from Mickey's Clubhouse. He'd been watching the show for as long as he could remember. When he was little, it was his favorite. He still liked to watch it sometimes, but would never admit it to his friends. Lisa said he was way too old to still be watching something like this. At Disney's Hollywood Studios, they had a live show kind of like a Mickey's Clubhouse episode at *Disney Junior's Live on Stage*. When he asked Lisa if she'd like to see it with him, she said she wouldn't be caught dead in that place.

Thankfully, his mom didn't feel the same way. He'd forgotten where Lisa and Dad had gone instead. Seeing the show on TV now, reminded him of the stage show, which was done with big puppets. He really liked it, even though you could see the wires moving their arms around. And he did feel a little old sitting there with so many little kids. But it was still fun.

The episode on TV, like all the others, was totally familiar. Instead of boring him, he felt...comforted. Mickey was using the Mystery Mouse-ka-tool right now to find something. Tootles, a flying thing shaped like a Mickey-head was buzzing around Mickey. Pleasant kid-music played in the background. Oh, no.

Mickey just said they needed Tootles to help them find Pluto's missing bouncing ball. Pluto was Mickey's dog. Now Mickey and Pluto were flying somewhere in a plane. Mickey called him his copilot and Pluto barked something in reply. They were looking over the sides of the plane for Pluto's ball.

Suddenly, all Jeffrey could think about was Riley. Riley was missing. He was way more important than a stupid bouncing ball. He was out there in the woods right now. Far, far away. Lost and alone. Jeffrey remembered how this cartoon ended. The same way they all ended. Their very small, make-believe problem gets solved, the same way they all do—with the help of Tootles and Mouse-ka-tools and a few other Disney characters who come by. They dance and sing the "Hot-Diggety-Dog" song together as the episode ends and everyone skips merrily away. Mickey appears and says, "See ya real soon." And it's over.

But that's not what's going to happen in Jeffrey's life. There was no Tootles or Mouse-ka-tool he could call on to help. No plane he could fly in to search for Riley. No little friends were going to come by to help him with the search. There was no little song or dance he could sing to make everything feel all better.

He had to shut off this TV show. Now. It wasn't taking his mind off anything. It was making everything worse. He zeroed in on the remote, sitting on top of the TV stand. It became blurry as tears welled up in his eyes. "Mom?" he cried. "Can you come here? Please."

She quickly rushed in. "What's the matter? Are you okay? Aww, you're crying. Your leg hurting?"

"It's hurting some, but that's not why I'm crying." He pointed to the TV. She looked in time to see Pluto sitting beside Mickey, a big grin on his face.

For half a second, she looked confused. Then she understood. "You're missing Riley." She reached for the remote. He nodded. "Want me to change the channel or turn it off?"

"You can turn it off. I'm pretty tired." He wiped his eyes. "Is Dad coming to get me soon?"

"In just a few minutes." She walked over and sat on the edge of the sofa, brushed the hair off his forehead. "I'm so sorry about Riley, and about your foot. Not a very nice way to end a Disney vacation."

"No, it's not. Mom, what are we going to do? How are we ever going to find him? A couple of weeks ago I watched a movie about some kids who lost their dog. They did all kinds of things to get him back. Like make posters, and put them on telephone poles all around the area where he got lost. They called dog shelters in case anyone who found him dropped him off. But we can't do any of those things with Riley. We lost him in the woods. There aren't any telephone poles anywhere around, not even any towns with dog shelters nearby. If somebody finds him, because of the stupid thing I did, they won't even know he's our dog." He burst into tears.

She reached over and hugged him gently. "What do you mean, the stupid thing you did?"

"I hooked his leash to the skinny little ring that holds his dog tag on, instead of the bigger ring on his collar. That's why he got away. When he went after that rabbit, the ring broke. So not only is he lost in the woods, but if anyone finds him, they won't know who he is, or who he belongs to." He cried even harder. Everything seemed so hopeless.

For a few moments, Mom didn't say anything. Then she said quietly, "I know something we can do."

"What?"

"We can't see Riley, and we don't know where he is. But God sees everything. He knows right where Riley is at this very moment. Maybe we should hold hands and pray for God to protect him, and somehow bring him back to us safe and sound."

Jeffrey stopped crying. "Do you think it could work?"

"I do. I know you go to Kid's church on Sundays, so you don't hear what our pastor says. Last Sunday, before we went on our trip, he read the story in the Bible about when Jesus came to earth. The pastor went through one miracle after another that God did to make the birth of Christ happen, just the way God predicted it would hundreds of years before Christmas night."

"It would have to be a miracle for Riley to get found *and* be brought back to us," Jeffrey said, as new tears rolled down his cheeks.

She reached for his hand. He gave it to her. "Then that's what we'll pray for, a miracle."

25

It was a cold, wet morning.

Again.

John was sitting by the main fire, all bundled up. He didn't want to get out of the sack this morning. Not because he was sleeping so well or so comfortably, but because he didn't want to face the day. He'd sunk into a deep depression the last few days, ever since that fellow Wilkins got crushed in his tent by that tree limb. It wasn't that he missed Wilkins. John wasn't sure they ever had one conversation together. It was what Wilkins' death represented. What happened to him could've happened to anyone in this camp. Including John.

It could've happened yesterday afternoon or evening, in fact. A fresh thunderstorm had rolled through, bringing all his fears back to the surface. The booming thunder, the flashes of lightning, the drenching downpour. The realization that he was totally helpless for every minute the storm lasted. No place to go. No place to hide. Just lay there in your tent, trembling till the horror faded.

"Some coffee?"

John looked up. It was Alfred. He took the cup. "Thanks." Alfred was safe to be around when he felt like this. He knew better than to try to talk John out of it.

"No more thunderstorms in the forecast," Alfred said. "Maybe we'll get a chance to dry out, and I can try to reapply that weatherproofing stuff on the tent."

John nodded, sipped the coffee.

Jenny came up, took a seat next to Alfred. "Fire feels good." She sipped her coffee, too.

"You doing any better?" Alfred asked. "I mean, about your friend? The guy who died?"

"A little. The funeral was yesterday. Supposed to bring closure, I guess. That's what they say anyway. We'll see."

John hoped they stopped talking about this soon. Else, he'd have to head back to the tent.

Alfred seemed to pick up on this. "Can you believe it? Christmas is one week from today. Think we'll have a white one?"

Jenny laughed. "I don't think so. I just hope it's a dry one. That's all I'm asking Santa for this year."

Here-here, John thought.

"Your tent got any leaks?" Alfred said.

"No, thank the good Lord. What, you guys got leaks?"

"A couple. But the way that rain's been coming down the last two times, a couple leaks is a couple too many."

"I hear ya."

"You hungry, John?" he asked.

John shook his head no. He felt like being alone, so he stood to take his leave. "Heading back to the tent. Guess I'll hang a few things out to dry."

"What's the hurry?" Alfred said as he walked away.

The hurry was to stop listening to them yakking about thunderstorms. Besides, if the storms really had moved on, he might as well get some things out in the fresh air. That was one good thing about Florida, when it wasn't raining, things on the line tended to dry out pretty good.

He was about halfway through his laundry pile when he heard something moving in the bushes behind their tent. He stopped to listen. Was it some kind of animal? He had a baseball bat just inside the tent. Should he go get it? Nothing happened. Maybe it was all in his head.

He started hanging things up again, had just set clothespins on the last long sleeve shirt when he heard that same rustling sound again. He stopped, looked. Again, nothing. Should he walk over there? Not without the bat. That wouldn't be smart.

Feeling kind of spooked by this, he picked up his coffee mug and started walking back to the main fire. Whatever it was would hopefully go away.

Two minutes later, he saw Alfred and Jenny still sitting in their same chairs. He hoped they'd found better things to talk about. Or maybe they had stopped talking altogether. He could use a few moments' peace.

"Would you look at that?" Jenny said, looking his way.

What was she talking about?

"Well, I'll be…" Alfred said, same surprised expression on

his face. "Don't look now, John, but you're being followed."

"What? What is it?"

"Nothing to worry about," Jenny said. "Just a dog. A little black dog walking about ten steps behind you."

"Got some white in it, looks like," Alfred said.

John turned around. There it was, right behind him. It stopped when he stopped. Poor thing, looked soaking wet. So that's what he'd heard back at the tent.

"What's a dog doing way out here?" Alfred said.

"Well, look at him," Jenny said. "He's obviously lost. He's soakin,' wringin' wet. Well, wait a minute. Maybe it's a her and not a him." She took a look. "No, definitely a him."

"He's gotta be lost if he's following John," Alfred said.

John actually smiled at that. The dog sat. Its head, which had been drooping, now lifted slightly. He looked right at him. John could tell it wasn't a mean dog, just by his eyes. He looked about as scared as John felt inside. John squatted, held out his hand. "Hey, boy," he said kindly. "What you doing out here in the woods by yourself?"

The dog's tail wagged momentarily. Slowly, he moved toward John's hand. Then stopped about two feet away.

"That dog's got no discernment at all," Alfred said.

"Stop," Jenny whispered. "Don't want to scare him off."

"Either of you got some food?" John said softly, but kept his gaze on the dog. Tried to make his face look pleasant.

"Got a bunch of tater tots in my pocket."

"In your pocket?" Jenny said.

"I like to snack on 'em while I drink my coffee."

"That's even more disgusting, washing those things down with coffee."

"Bring a few here," John said. "Put them in my hand." He held one hand behind his back, the palm upturned. "Walk slowly."

Alfred did, then walked backwards and stood by his chair.

John held out one of the tater tots toward the dog. Its tail immediately started to wag again. "Come on, come on and get it. It's okay."

The dog obeyed. He took the tot in his mouth gently but gobbled it down in a flash, then he sat.

"Want some more?" John held out another. Once again, the dog almost swallowed it whole.

"Poor thing," Jenny said. "Probably hasn't eaten for days."

John held out a third tater tot, but this time kept it closer so that the dog had to come his way a little. It did without hesitation. This time, John held the tater tot in between two fingers and said, "Take it, gently." Just to see if it would.

"Look at that," Jenny said.

It reached for the tater tot much more slowly, licked it first, then John released it. The dog actually chewed it this time.

As it did, John patted its head. "That's a good boy." When he looked at the palm of his hand, it was covered in mud. The missing mud revealed a big white spot on top of the dog's head.

He gave the dog the final tater tot, but this time gently took hold of his collar. "Alfred, go into the tent and get me that short piece of rope you have. The one you tie around your suitcase when you travel."

"What do you need it for?"

"He's gonna make a leash, silly."

"Think that's a good idea. Keeping it on a leash? Maybe it likes roaming free."

"Just do it," John said. "A dog like this has probably never been free a day in its life. We're homeless on purpose. This little guy has no idea how to live out here." Alfred headed toward the tent. As John looked at the dog's coat more closely, he saw a lot more mud clinging to it. He brushed some of the bigger clots off. "Look at this. More white spots. This isn't a black dog. It's just a dog that needs a good bath."

"He's got a collar on," Jenny said. "See if he's got a dog tag. If he's somebody's pet, people usually put their info on tags."

John felt around the collar. "No tag." The dog seemed to relax more, the more John handled it.

"You know what might have happened," Alfred said as he walked up with the rope. "It's a sad thing, but it does happen. It would explain how a pet-quality dog like him got stuck out here in the woods all by himself, with no dog tag or ID."

"What are you talking about?" Jenny said.

He handed the rope to John. "He got dumped out here on purpose. Some people do that. The dog gets on their nerves, maybe it barks too much or causes some other kind of trouble, and they get tired of it."

"So they drive out to the middle of nowhere and turn the dog loose in the woods?" Jenny said.

"It happens. Least that way the dog gets a fighting chance to survive. They bring it down to the pound and it gets euthanized. Nobody wants somebody else's old dog."

"You sound like you've got some experience with this sort of thing," Jenny said.

"What, me? I'd never do that to a dog. But I know a guy who did. Happens all the time."

"Well, however it got here," John said, "it's here now. We need to get it some fresh water, some more food and get him cleaned up." He tied the rope on tightly to its collar then made something of a handle with the other end. He stood and the dog stood with him, right next to his side.

"Look at that," Jenny said. "He heeled and you didn't even tell him to."

Alfred reached over and handed him his last two tater tots. The dog instantly sat and took them very politely.

"What a good boy you are," John said in a very different voice than anyone had ever heard before.

Hearing that, the dog's tail wagged faster than it had so far. His mouth opened slightly and his tongue stuck out, almost like he was panting. Only he wasn't panting.

"What a cute face he's making," Jenny said. "Almost looks like he's smiling, doesn't it?"

The dog's ears instantly perked up, and he cocked his head as he looked at Jenny.

"Wonder what that's about?" Alfred said.

"I don't know," she said. "He did it when I said *smiling*."

"There he goes again." The dog cocked his head the other way.

"He seems to like that word," John said. "Maybe that's

what we'll call him…Smiley."

He looked right up at John, wagged his tail some more and smiled.

John pat his head and rubbed his ears. "Smiley, it is. Okay Smiley, let's get you fed and cleaned up."

John walked toward the food tent holding Smiley's makeshift leash. The dog walked right beside him in a perfect heel.

26

The woman he had just met put a bowl in front of him. Before it even reached the ground, Riley knew what it was. Some had splashed over the sides. WATER! Fresh water in a bowl, not moving. Nothing floating by. He was beginning to wonder if he'd ever get water like this again. He lapped it up as fast as he could swallow.

"Look at the poor thing," Jenny said. "Must have been dying of thirst."

"I don't know how," Alfred said. "All that rain we been having. Puddles of water are lying around everywhere."

"Puddles?" she repeated. "I'd like to see you drink water out of a puddle. I imagine a wild dog wouldn't care, but one raised in a home since being a pup...they'd probably struggle just as much as you."

Riley's belly was just about full. He heard them talking but didn't recognize any of the words. He was already glad he took a chance on these people. He'd wandered around the woods all morning smelling all kinds of smells and hearing all kinds of different noises. None of them familiar. He'd gotten so hungry he started chasing anything that moved. A rabbit, a squirrel, even lizards. But he couldn't catch a thing.

He wasn't sure what that man had just fed him, but he would happily eat more or anything else that remotely resembled the food he used to get back home.

He stopped drinking and sat. Water dripped down his chin. For a moment, he felt nervous but then realized he was outside, not on the kitchen floor. His insides started to feel almost normal. If only he could get more food. He could smell some nearby. How could he make them understand he was hungry?

"Looks like he's done drinking," John said. He bent down and picked up the bowl. "You think anyone here would mind if I borrow this for a few days, bring it back to our tent?"

"I'm sure that's fine," Jenny said. "It's just an old metal bowl, not part of a matched set. Did you notice how the dog reacted when you took the bowl away?"

"He didn't react," John said.

"Right. That means something. He doesn't have resource aggression. That's a good thing."

"Resource aggression?" Alfred said. "You just make that up?"

"No, I didn't just make that up. A couple of years ago I got sentenced to thirty hours' community service. Did my time volunteering at a Humane Society. It was in a different county, over on the Gulf coast. Anyway, they used to test dogs that people brought in, to make sure they weren't aggressive. When a dog growled or snapped at someone if you got near their food or water, they'd call it resource aggression. And while I'm explaining things, let me clear up something else you said a few minutes ago, Alfred. About your friend dumping his dog off in the woods so it wouldn't get euthanized at a shelter. That's kind of a bum rap most of these dog shelters get. The one I worked at only put dogs to sleep as a last resort. Like if they were aggressive or potentially dangerous. It was always a sad thing, even then. I told them I couldn't be a part of it. But I understood why after working there a bit. Can't send a dog out to the public that's gonna bite people. You gotta think about that, especially about the kids."

"The dumping thing wasn't my idea," Alfred said. "I'm just telling you what my friend said."

"Well, your friend's an idiot. And if he dropped his dog off in the woods on purpose he should be locked up."

"If I see him, I'll be sure to pass on your message."

Riley sat patiently, listening to them talk. He wasn't sure if they were talking about him, but they kept looking at him the whole time. He was *so* hungry. Maybe if he did a trick. Jeffrey always gave him treats when he did tricks. Still sitting, he lifted his two front paws up as high as he could and held them there for as long as he could. Jeffrey liked that one. His mom especially did.

"Aww, look at him," Jenny said. "How adorable."

John smiled. "I think he's begging. Let's stop yakking and get him some food." They were close to the food tent. John looked over and saw a stack of dishes with bits of different food no one had scraped off yet.

Alfred saw it, too. "Looks like the dishes for a few late-comers to breakfast haven't been cleaned up yet. We could get him something from that."

"Thinking the same thing. C'mon, boy. You hungry? Want something to eat?" John and Alfred walked toward the stack of dishes.

Hungry and *eat*. Riley liked the sound of that. He cheerfully followed the man holding his leash. At least, it looked like a leash.

"Here, you hold this, and I'll get him a plate." John gave Alfred the rope handle. "Don't let him go."

Jenny walked up behind them. "Don't give him any bread or toast. Just protein. Some dogs are allergic to wheat. Makes them itch something awful."

"Aren't those tater tots wheat?" Alfred said.

Jenny looked at him. "Alfred, think about it. *Tater* tots? What are taters?"

"Oh, yeah." He turned to John. "Put some of them on the plate. We know he likes them."

"I'm gonna put some of them in a baggy for later," John said. "To use as treats. I want to see what kinds of things this dog knows. There's plenty of scrambled eggs here and bits of sausage left." He looked down at the dog, who was staring right up at him. "You like these?" He held a piece of sausage link in front of his nose. His ears perked right up and his tail began to wag. "Take it nice."

Riley could hardly believe it. That piece of meat tasted as good as anything he had ever eaten. Was more of that coming?

He wanted to jump up on the man, to see what he was doing, but he knew he wasn't supposed to. Back home, his family had brought in someone to work with him several times about all kinds of things people wanted and didn't want him to do. Jumping was one, so he resisted the urge, as hard as it was, and remained in a sit.

"Look how excited he is," Jenny said. "He's vibrating."

"Almost done, boy," John said. "One more minute."

"John, that's too much." Jenny pointed at the plate. "Take some off. His stomach's probably empty. You don't want him to throw it all up five minutes after he eats."

"I guess you're right." John did what she said then showed it to her. "How's that?"

"That looks fine. Let's take it back to the fire, have him eat there. Or maybe at your tent. It's a good idea to have him eat at the same place each time. Don't want him to get used to eating here."

"Okay. Alfred, you hold the food. I'll walk Smiley. Let's go to our tent."

The three of them started walking away. Riley eagerly followed, and not because he was on a leash.

The smells coming off that plate were amazing.

27

An hour later, John, Alfred and Jenny were sitting in chairs in front of John and Alfred's tent. The dog they'd been calling Smiley was now sleeping soundly at John's feet. He had eaten every bite of the breakfast plate John had fixed then licked the plate clean. Alfred said it looked so clean, John could put it right back in circulation.

Next, Jenny had given him a bath while John and Alfred looked on. John had started out doing it, but Jenny pushed him aside saying he wasn't scrubbing hard enough. Through it all, Riley was as pleasant as could be.

"Seeing him all cleaned up," Jenny said, "that is one beautiful dog. Know what he reminds me of?"

"See Spot run?" John said.

"Run Spot run," Alfred added.

They all laughed.

"Spittin' image of that little dog in our first grade reader," Jenny said. "Kinda crazy that we all remember that. But I guess we are all about the same age."

"Gonna be hard for ole Spot here to run," Alfred said, "you keep him all tied up like that. Don't you think?" He was looking at John.

"First off, he's not all tied up. This rope is just taking the place of a leash, which we don't have. And second, some dogs need to be on a leash whenever they're outside, or else in a fenced in yard." In an exaggerated way he took a slow pan of their surroundings. "Last I checked, we don't have any fences here."

"How do you know he'll run off if you turn him loose?"

"Because I know. He's that kind of dog. Some dogs are bred to be real homebodies. They'll stick around their own property even without a fence. And they'll walk right next to their owners without a leash. Smiley here, isn't one of them. He's got that built-in instinct to run off. He can't help himself. He's got that...what do you call it, Jenny?"

"A prey drive. That's what they called it at the shelter. John's right, Alfred. Some dogs are just hardwired that way. They might like their owners just fine, and be plenty obedient in all other kinds of ways. But if they see something off in the distance, like a small animal, the urge to chase after it is overpowering. Probably how this sweet fella got lost."

"This rope is for his own good," John said. He really meant it, but secretly he was also glad to have this as an excuse. He'd only been with them an hour or two, but John was already liking having the little guy around.

A chair squeaked loudly, interrupting Riley's dream. He lifted his head and looked around. Took a minute to realize where he was. The three people who had begun to take care of him were still there.

The lady had just stood. "Sorry little guy, did I wake you?"

John reached down and patted his head. "Going somewhere?"

"Looks like you guys have everything in hand," Jenny said. "I've got some Christmas chores to tend to, with the big day being only a week away."

"Christmas chores?" Alfred said. "Like what?"

"Well, I've gotta mail out my annual Christmas letter. I don't have enough money to mail everyone a fancy card, so I just write a one-page letter, go down to the office store and get copies made. But I have to mail each one separate since none of my relatives live close to each other."

Alfred shook his head. "I don't think I've sent or received a Christmas card since...I don't know...decades maybe. You stay close with your family?"

"Not close. It's pretty much just this Christmas letter each year."

"What kind of stuff do you say?"

"Not too much. Usually just ramble on about whatever comes to mind. Probably'll mention this cute little dog walking into our camp this morning. Stuff like that. The main thing is to let them know I'm still on the planet."

"Do they ever send you Christmas cards?" Alfred asked.

"Where would they send them?" John said. "Not like

there's a mailbox out by the street."

"Yeah, you're right. Forget I asked."

"How about you, John?" she asked. "You got any family you're still connected to."

"Nope. Parents passed away long time ago. Never been married. Had a younger brother. We stopped connecting years ago. Don't even know where he is. Christmas is just like any other day of the year to me."

"Well, maybe this year will be different," Alfred said. "Seeing who just wandered into our camp today. He hasn't taken his eyes off you ever since he woke up. Maybe for you Christmas came a week early."

John looked down at Riley. Riley had suspected they were talking about him at least part of the time, but he couldn't recognize anything they had said. Except for the word *dog*, which Riley knew the family sometimes used when they spoke about him. He sat up.

John scratched the top of his head. "Don't leave just yet, Jenny. You'll miss the show."

"Show?"

He pulled a baggy out of his jacket pocket, which instantly peaked Riley's curiosity. He couldn't smell what was inside, but they looked just like the tasty things he was given when he first entered the camp.

"I'm gonna see what kinds of tricks he knows."

Jenny leaned up against a tree. "I suppose that's worth waiting for."

Riley's eyes were fixed on that baggy. He came around in

front of the man to get a better look. He still wasn't sure of his name.

"You can try, but I doubt he knows any tricks," Alfred said. "The kind of guy that dumps a dog out in the woods, ain't the kind of guy who'll take time to work with a dog."

"Well, let's just see then." John pulled the tater tot out of the bag and held it in front of the dog's face.

By its smell and the way it looked, Riley instantly knew what it was. He was prepared to do whatever the man asked.

"Sit, Smiley. Sit."

Okay, *sit*. Riley knew that. He waited for the proper hand signal, but it didn't come. That was okay. Maybe the man didn't know it. He sat anyway.

"Good boy. Did you see that?" John handed him the tater tot adding the word *gently*.

"Well, every dog knows sit," Alfred said.

"See if he knows *shake*," Jenny said.

Riley looked at the woman. He knew the word she said. Should he go over to her? Just then, the man took out another treat.

John held the second tater tot out. "Smiley, shake. Shake, Smiley."

Again, no hand signal. But Riley instantly handed the man his left paw. Or did he want the other one? He changed paws. Maybe he wanted both. Riley lifted both of them in the air and held them there.

"Look at that," Jenny said. "Talk about eager to please. And look at that expression on his face. Looks like he's smiling."

"I guess that qualifies as a shake," John said. "And then some." He gave the dog the tater tot. He took it gently without being asked.

Then John asked him to lie down. He obeyed immediately. He asked him to roll over and spun the tater tot in a circular motion. Again, the dog obeyed. Wagging his tail the whole time. He asked him to sit, then held his palm out and said, "Stay." John got out of his chair and walked back to the tent. The dog didn't move. His eyes remained focused on John. "Okay, come." He instantly came and gently took the final tater tot.

"Wow," Alfred said. "I never knew a dog who did all that. He's good-lookin' and smart."

John reached over and gave the dog a big hug. "What a good boy you are, Smiley."

Riley was really enjoying this. But it instantly reminded him of fun times he'd had with Jeffrey. He had learned how to do all these things with Jeffrey and this nice lady who kept coming by the house. That lady was special. She really seemed to understand him. Then she stopped coming, but Jeffrey kept doing these routines with him for the next several weeks. After that, he only did them every now and then. Like, when guests would come over to the house. Jeffrey would have Riley sit right in front of him and run through everything he had learned. Each time, giving him treats just like this man did. Telling him what a good boy he was, and giving him hugs.

Just like this man was doing now. Was he supposed to be with this man from now on, in this place? Would he ever see Jeffrey or the family again?

28

John had gone about his day as normally as possible. Of course, with Smiley by his side that proved to be something of a challenge. It wasn't really the dog's fault. He seemed to be very easygoing and didn't present any real difficulties, except that word had spread throughout the camp and all day long people kept stopping by to greet him.

By the end of the day, one thing was abundantly clear: Smiley loved people, of all shapes and sizes. It seemed to John, Smiley hadn't met a single person in camp he didn't like. The only problem was…John didn't like most people, in general, and he liked being the center of so much attention even less.

Another guy John had never even talked to before had just left their tent site, after sharing with John all of his expertise in the field of dog care and maintenance.

"I don't know how much more of this advice and goodwill I can take," John said.

"It'll die down in a day or so," Alfred said. "People are just curious. And you can tell from what kinds of things they were saying, most of them had a dog at one time in their life. And the way they talked about their dog memories, almost all of them were good. That's what seeing Smiley means to 'em. Conjuring up better times than the time they're in now. Didn't you ever have a dog, John? Seems like you must have, the way you been handling him all day."

John instantly flashed back to the Christmas morning when he was ten years old. He'd been asking his folks for a dog all year, but they had always said he was too young to have one. He and his younger brother had already opened up the few Christmas presents his parents could afford and John was trying to act excited and grateful for what they did receive. But it was hard to stop thinking about the one thing he did want that wasn't under the tree.

A puppy.

Just then his father had gotten up from his favorite chair, saying he had to go to the bathroom. He returned two minutes later holding a big unwrapped box, set it right in front of John. "What is it?" John heard a noise coming from inside. A pawing sound and some whimpering. Just as he'd opened the top flap, the box fell over. Pushed over, is more accurate. A soft, brown puppy came spilling out onto his lap. He was jumping all over John, licking him from head to toe. John hugged the little guy tight and thanked his mom and dad over and over again, declaring this the best Christmas he'd ever had.

And it was. He'd named the pup Astro, like the dog on his favorite Saturday morning cartoon, the Jetsons.

"John?"

John cleared his head, looked at Alfred. "Yes, I did. My dog was the best friend I ever had growing up."

"Then you get why everyone stopping by is so happy to see this little guy."

"I guess you're right."

"Course I'm right. Have you thought about what you're gonna feed him for dinner? Where he's gonna sleep tonight?"

John looked down at Smiley lying by his feet, half-asleep. "No. I don't have a plan here. This whole thing just kinda happened."

"I know. But don't you think we should figure some things out? Starting with, are we gonna keep him?"

"I don't know. Doesn't seem like we got much choice for the moment. Can't hardly toss him back out in the woods. He'd die of starvation or thirst in a few days. He doesn't have an ID tag on his collar. Seems like if he had a decent owner, they would have put one on him, so he could be returned if he got lost. The fact that he has a collar, but no tag, lends some support to your crazy idea that someone just dumped him out here in the woods to be rid of him. But he's such a nice dog, that hardly makes any sense."

"I hear ya'. So what are we gonna do?"

They both heard footsteps and looked up to see Hampton heading their way. He was one of the two guys who'd started the camp.

"This ought to be interesting," Alfred said.

Riley lifted his head to greet yet another person coming his way. A tall man with a beard. Lots of the men around here had beards. This man's beard was a little darker. He was smiling. Thankfully, all the people he'd met today seemed happy to see him.

"So, there he is. Thought I'd come over and check out this new fellow that's causing all the excitement around camp today."

"Hey, Hampton," Alfred said. "Yep, he's guilty as charged."

Hampton walked up slowly and bent down. "He got a name?"

"Didn't have tag on," John said. "So, we're not sure what his name is. We've been calling him Smiley."

"On account of the face he makes most the time," Alfred said. "You'll see it in a sec. He gets relaxed, looks just like he's smiling."

Hampton reached out his hand as if to pet him. "Everybody says he's a friendly dog."

"Go ahead," John said. "He won't bite. Doesn't seem to have a mean bone in his body."

Hampton did, then scratched between his ears and under his chin.

Riley wagged his tail. Although, greeting so many people in so short a time was making him tired. And hungry.

"So, he just walked in here right out of the woods? A dog that looks like this?"

"Well, he didn't look like that when he came outta the woods," Alfred said. "He was so muddy we thought he was a black dog at first. We gave him a bath. Well, Jenny did. But yeah, he just showed up. John was walking down the path toward the main fire, and I looked up and saw this dog following him."

"I actually heard him a few minutes before that," John said, "making some noise in the bushes behind our tent. Thought it was some kind of animal, like a raccoon or something."

Hampton gently grabbed his collar, lifted his head to see it better. Spun it around.

"Ain't no ID tag," Alfred said. "We figured someone must've just dumped him out in the woods to get rid of him. Maybe off that highway…what's that one a few miles west of here?"

"301," Hampton said. "Guess that could be. Seems crazy someone would dump a nice looking dog like this. And one so good-natured."

"Some people are just selfish jerks," Alfred said.

"You guys plan to keep him?"

Alfred looked at John. "Ask him. Seems like the dog's picked him out as his new owner. He likes me fine, but you can see who he's chosen to sit by. Been following John around all day."

Hampton looked at the leash John was holding in his hand. "Seems like he's got no choice, you got him on a leash like that."

"I only got him on a leash, so he don't run off again. He was half starving when we found him."

"Jenny used to work with dogs," Alfred said. "You can talk

to her about it. She says dogs like him don't run off 'cause they want to, but because their instincts force them to. What did she call it, John?"

"Prey driven."

"Right. That's the only reason we got him on a leash. But I'm telling you, that leash has been slack all day. He hasn't pulled on it once. He's next to John because that's where he wants to be."

The man who had been petting him, stood again. Riley wasn't sure what it was, but the man seemed tense. He was pretty sure by now the one holding his leash was named John. He could sense John tensing up, too, the more this man talked.

"You asked a moment ago," John said, "whether we were planning on keeping the dog."

"Right. So, are you?"

"Alfred was asking me the same thing. We haven't gotten that far or made any real plans. Smiley just showed up here six or eight hours ago. I like him. He seems like a really nice dog. But at the moment, we're just trying to be kind to him. Take care of him, because he's lost and hungry. Seemed like the Christian thing to do, you know? But if I, or we, decided we wanted to keep him, could we? What are the rules? I haven't seen any other dogs in the camp since I've been here. Are they allowed?"

"Well, you know we don't have any rules written down here, John. We like to keep things live and let live, as much as possible. I don't know why there aren't any dogs in camp, to be honest with you. I guess most folks just travel light and don't want to have to worry about taking care of a dog, living out here like this. I'm mostly here to check things out, respond to complaints I've been getting."

"Complaints?" John said. "Who's been complaining? About this dog? What's there to complain about? I don't think I've heard him bark all day. He pooped once, but we bagged that real quick. Must've been twenty different people stop by here today, he's treated every one of them like they were good friends."

Riley could tell...John was downright upset now. Something this man was saying was making him angry. He sat up and leaned his head against John's leg, trying to comfort him. He felt John rest his hand lightly on his head.

"To be honest, John. They're not those kinds of complaints. I can see for myself he's a nice dog, and I can see even now, the way he's taken to you. But I had to come by and check, just so I could say I did."

"Well, what were people saying?"

"Looking at things now, I'm thinking they were maybe just a little jealous."

"About what?"

"Some were saying they didn't think you were much of a dog person, and a dog that nice ought to be with somebody who loved dogs. Some others were saying they might like to have a dog like this one, and didn't think it was right that you were acting like you owned it already. Thought maybe we should have a raffle."

"A raffle," Alfred said. "For crying out loud."

"Look, I'm just trying to keep the peace. I think a raffle's a lousy idea. You seem fine with the dog. And if it's like Alfred said, the dog picked you out of everyone else in this camp to turn to. So if you guys are willing to take responsibility for this dog, and he stays as nice as he seems to be, I say leave well enough alone."

Riley sensed the man's tone change, felt John begin to relax again. He wished he knew what they were talking about. Felt almost certain it was about him.

"So," Hampton said, "are we good?"

Alfred nodded.

"John? We good?"

John nodded also.

"Okay, then. You fellas have a good night. Just do me a favor, and keep a low profile around here for a few days. Can you do that? I'll talk to the people who complained, see if I can't get them to simmer down and give you guys a chance."

29

Savannah, Georgia

Four more days had passed, and still no word about Riley. Jeffrey passed the time moping about on the couch, watching TV or playing video games. He was still on his crutches and couldn't put any weight on his injured foot, but at least it didn't hurt that much anymore. Not unless he banged it. And he was getting pretty good moving about on his crutches.

The front door opened, and his father walked in. "I'm home. Off until the day after Christmas."

"Oh, hi Dad." Jeffrey waived. "Get any calls about Riley?"

Dad took off his coat, set it and his brief bag on an upholstered chair. "Sorry, no I didn't."

"Figured you probably didn't, or else you would've called."

Dad walked over and sat on the opposite edge of the couch. "How's the leg?"

"About the same. Did those dog tag people ever get back with you?"

"You mean about updating Riley's information, so that if anybody finds him that chip will connect them back to us?"

Jeffrey nodded.

"Only to say they got my email. I paid them the fee, gave them our new address and phone number, and my new email address. The lady said we're all set. If someone finds him, and they bring him somewhere that can scan the chip, they would definitely contact us." He looked around the living area. "Where's your mom and sister?"

"Mom's in the kitchen finishing up dinner. I think she's on the phone. Lisa's up in her room doing I don't know what."

His dad looked at him, sighed and gently placed his hand on Jeffrey's good leg. "There's something I need to talk to you about, before we eat dinner."

Jeffrey had paused his game but now set his controller down. "What is it?"

"Got a call from your mom at lunchtime. She and Lisa wanted me to talk to you about setting up our Christmas tree tonight. I know you've been wanting us to wait until Riley comes home but...Jeffrey, Christmas is in three days. The tree's been sitting there in the garage since we came home. Some of the needles are starting to fall off."

Jeffrey didn't want to talk about this. "Can't we just wait one more day?"

"But why? One more day's not going to make any difference."

"It might. Riley's always been there when we set up the tree, as long as I can remember. And he always makes it so much fun."

"I know, son. And I want him to come home just as much as you do. We all want Riley home. But we have to keep going forward. The rest of the family really wants to set the tree up tonight and to start enjoying this holiday a little bit."

"You want to set the tree up too?"

Dad nodded his head yes. "Can I ask why you don't want to do it?"

Tears welled up in his eyes. "Because then it's like saying Riley's never coming home. Like we're giving up on ever seeing him again."

His dad reached over and gave him a hug. "It's okay to cry." He didn't say anything for a few moments. "You know, you can miss Riley and still try to enjoy Christmas, right? Setting up the tree doesn't mean we're giving up hope."

"It feels like it to me."

"I know. But it's just a feeling, son. You've got it in your head somehow that one thing is connected to the other, but they're not. If Riley comes home, it'll be a wonderful thing. But if he doesn't, it won't be because we set the Christmas tree up tonight. Can you see what I'm saying?"

"I guess so."

"Tell you what, you think about what I said over dinner, and we'll talk about it again after. Is that all right?"

Jeffrey nodded.

Two hours later, the family was sitting around the living room decorating the tree. Dad had just finished replacing some of the faulty lights. Mom had the Christmas music playing in the background. They always listened to the same playlist, made by Mom several years ago. A mix of Johnny Mathis, Bing Crosby, Josh Groban and Michael Buble.

Jeffrey was doing his best to suppress any memories of Riley and all the little mischievous things he did trying to help them decorate the tree. He wasn't just a member of the family; to Jeffrey, he was the most fun member.

After selecting the Disney ornament Jeffrey had gotten on their vacation, he carefully walked it back to the tree.

"Don't put it there, Jeffrey," Lisa said. "That middle section of the tree already has too many."

"Well, I can't reach the top half, or my crutches will fall off."

"Here, point to where you want it, and I'll hang it."

Jeffrey backed up a step and did what she suggested.

"How's that?"

"Fine," he said. "But are we gonna do this every time until we're done?"

"Here," Mom said. She slid a leather ottoman over by one section of the tree near the wall. "This part of the tree is bare. Why don't you rest your legs a little while and sit here?" She set a box of larger ornaments next to it. "You can use these."

Jeffrey leaned his crutches against the wall and sat on the ottoman. It did feel good to take a break. But sitting there, he noticed something. They were almost done decorating the tree. He immediately remembered what usually came next. "Can I ask you guys a favor? I know we have all these traditions, but could we skip one tonight. Maybe start another one instead?"

"What are you talking about?" Lisa said.

"Usually after we're done setting the tree, Mom makes us all hot chocolate and we sit around watching old family videos of Christmases when we were younger."

"Why can't we do that?" Lisa said. "I like that tradition. I vote no, that we don't change it. Why do you want to change it anyway? What do you want to do instead?"

"I'm trying not to think about how much I miss Riley. He's in every one of those old videos."

"Hmmm," Dad said. "I forgot about that."

"I'm open to that," Mom said. "What would you like to do instead?"

"Well I'm not open to that," Lisa said. "Don't I get a say in this? I like watching those old family videos. It's the only time we ever do it."

"Lisa, think about what your brother's going through for once," Dad said. "Not just what you want. He's having a harder time with losing Riley than you are. I think we should try and help him out." He looked at Jeffrey. "What would you want to do instead?"

"I don't know. Maybe we could watch a Christmas movie together."

"Like what?" Mom said. "Which one?"

"I don't know. How about that one you're always asking Lisa and me to watch every year. That black and white one about the guy who jumps off a bridge."

"It's a Wonderful Life?" Dad said.

"That's the one," Jeffrey said. "We could watch that one."

"I think that's a great idea," Dad said. "That's still my favorite Christmas movie of all time. I think you guys would love it if you gave it a chance."

"I don't want to see an old black and white movie," Lisa said. "Why can't we just do what we do every year? We could just fast forward through any parts that have Riley in it."

"That won't help," Jeffrey said. "I'll still see him, even if the pictures are moving fast."

"Well, what's so wrong with that? I don't even understand why it bothers you so much to see him. You should make something positive out of it. Like when you see him, think about all the good times you've had, rather than trying to pretend he doesn't exist."

"That's not what I'm trying to do."

"That's what it seems like to me. And all it's doing is making you sad. And…keeping the rest of us from being able to enjoy Christmas."

"You don't understand," he said.

"C'mon, you two," Mom said sternly.

"I'm not trying to be mean. I'm just trying to help Jeffrey get over this. We've all been walking around here the last few days, trying to avoid doing or saying anything about what happened. But we can't do anything about the situation. I don't blame you, Jeffrey, for losing Riley. If I was the one who'd taken him for a walk that day, I could have hooked his leash up wrong, too. It just happened. I think we need to accept it and try to make the best of it. Or else it's going to ruin our entire Christmas." She stopped talking a moment, and looked as if she'd just got a great idea. "You know...one thing we could do...it's something people do all the time at Christmas. Why don't we go down to the shelter tomorrow and pick out a new puppy?"

"Lisa," Dad said.

"What? I think it's a great idea."

Jeffrey stood, grabbed his crutches and shoved them under his arms. He started to cry. "I don't want a new puppy. I want Riley back." He quickly started hobbling toward the stairway.

"Jeffrey, come back," Mom said.

30

The last few days at the camp had gone pretty well for John. Smiley had won over all the critics just by being himself. John had won them over by pretending to be someone else.

That first night Smiley arrived, Alfred had offered John some good advice. *"If you want this thing with the dog to work out, I suggest you don't act on what you're probably feeling right now. For the next several days, don't lash out and pull away from everybody. Instead, prove them wrong. Get out there and show Smiley off. Let people see 'em and see you with him. Let them pet him some and make a general fuss over him. He'll win them over. And folks'll see how good you are with him, and all this rigga-marole about you not being a good fit for the dog'll die down."*

Surprisingly, it had worked, just as Alfred had predicted.

Even Hampton had come back yesterday after dinner to let John know things seemed much better around the camp, and that he was okay if John wanted to keep the dog around. He'd said a number of people had also mentioned how much their opinion of John had changed over the last several days, saying he seemed much more friendly and easier to be around.

John wasn't so sure this was a compliment, but Alfred had insisted it was.

Today, John had decided it was time to let things go back to the way they used to be. Meaning, he was all done with the *John-loves-to-be-around-people* act. Not that he was going to start treating people mean; just that he wasn't going out of his way anymore to maintain all this newfound goodwill. He liked the dog, and the dog seemed to like him. That was enough. Smiley was absolutely no trouble at all and, John had to admit, somehow just being around him had lifted John out of the depression-hole he'd fallen into a few days ago.

Right now, John was walking Smiley across the camp toward Jenny's site. They had just finished cleaning up after dinner. Once again, Riley's diet consisted of smaller portions of what he and Alfred had been eating. If he was gonna keep Smiley, it was high time to make some changes.

He rounded the corner and saw Jenny up ahead. Looked like she was adding a few more Christmas ornaments to a little palm tree that already had quite a few. Smiley got excited when he saw her and, of course, she made quite a scene when she turned and saw him. Big smile, hands clapping, calling out his name in a high-pitched happy voice. Smiley started yanking on the leash trying to close the gap more quickly.

"Okay Boy, slow it down." John yanked gently on the rope. Smiley quickly got the message and stopped pulling. But John could tell he was still majorly excited.

"To what do I owe this pleasure?" Jenny asked. She bent

down and opened her arms to receive Smiley. John let go of the rope when they were a few feet away. He lunged toward her and started licking her face. She laughed and hugged him and half-heartedly asked him to stop.

"Got a favor to ask," John said. "I see you're busy. Wasn't that palm tree already decorated?"

"I noticed a few bare spots. Can't have that with Christmas three days away. So, what's the favor?" Smiley had calmed down a bit, and was now sitting beside her.

"Do you still have that cell phone?"

"I do."

"Is it charged up?"

"Should be. Got it all charged up at the library a couple days ago. Haven't used it since. Let me go check." She looked at Smiley. "I'll be right back. You be good." She opened the flap and ducked inside her tent. A moment later, she was back, holding the phone in her hand. "Looks like it's still half-charged. Want to borrow it?"

"If you don't mind. As you can see, me and the dog are getting along pretty well. Folks at the camp seem to be accepting the idea of him being around. Thought it's time I should go to some pet supply store and get a few things to make his life a little more normal around here." He held up the rope. "Like exchanging this for a proper leash. Buy him some regular dog food. A regular dog bowl. Things like that."

"That sounds like a good idea. Maybe buy him a dog toy or two." She looked at Smiley. "For a Christmas present," she said in his direction, as if she was talking to a baby. "He's been such a good boy, haven't you?"

"I guess I could do that. If they don't cost too much."

"If you can only afford one, can I make a suggestion?"

"By all means. Since you worked at that shelter a while, I'd appreciate any advice you have."

"Now see, that sounds like the new John talking. People are saying how much this dog is improving your demeanor, and I'd have to agree. Here you are complimenting me and asking for my advice. And I'll tell you another thing, I've actually seen you smile several times the last few days. I don't think I've ever seen you smile before. You better watch out, or people around here will start calling you Smiley."

John laughed. He was starting to feel a little awkward. "Okay, so you were gonna tell me what dog toy to buy."

"Oh, right. If you can only buy one, I'd recommend a stuffed animal. Preferably, one with a good squeaker. Since Smiley's got that prey drive, I think that's probably the kind of toy he'd enjoy the most."

"I'll look into getting one of those."

"This is starting to sound expensive. Maybe you should try the Goodwill first instead of the pet store. You might find all this stuff there." She handed him the cell phone. "Now keep in mind, there's no signal out here. But you can pick one up not too far from here. You know that Baptist church on the right, a few blocks down? Apparently, they got a cell tower in their steeple or something. You can get a pretty decent signal on the outskirts of their property."

"Okay. I don't suppose you ever looked up the phone

number for a cab company."

"Got one right there in my favorites section. Here, I'll show you." She found it, showed it to him and handed the phone back. "What's your plan?"

"Well, come to think of it...I might need your help a little more. I don't suppose you could watch Smiley for me while I go make this call? Don't feel too good walking a few blocks next to the road with him on nothing more than this old rope."

"Are you kidding? I would love to watch him. Are you gonna have the cab pick you up closer to here?"

"Yeah, but I'm not going to have them come until tomorrow, around midmorning. I'm just gonna set things up now from that church property, then come back for the night. So I won't be gone for maybe a half-hour or so."

"Take your time. Don't rush back on account of me. Me and Smiley here will be doing just fine."

It took John closer to forty-five minutes, but he got a good signal and the call to the cab company went through okay. He was also glad that the church parking lot was empty. Didn't want anybody thinking he was some kind of prowler hanging around someplace after business hours. He walked back through the campsite, taking a bit more care with each step since it was starting to get dark.

When he neared Jenny's tent site, he saw her sitting in a chair next to her decorated-though-unlit palm tree reading a book. Her face glowed slightly from a little clip-on reading light. Smiley was lying by her feet. As John approached, Riley's head popped up and his tail started wagging. Then he stood. His front feet started prancing. He was actually excited to see John return. John was smiling as it dawned on him how good it felt.

Jenny looked up and saw him, too. But she didn't smile. If anything, she had a serious expression on her face. He wondered what was wrong.

Smiley yanked on the edge of his rope, trying to get to John. "Hey boy, how are you doing? You been good for Jenny?" He bent down and greeted him proper.

She set the book down on her lap. "He's been an absolute angel."

"Glad to hear it. Is everything okay?"

"What? Uh…yeah. Why do you ask?"

"It's just that, as I walked up you had a pretty stern look on your face."

"Did I?" She looked down at the book and sighed.

"You reading a depressing book?"

"No, not exactly." She paused, looked at John as though she had something to say.

"What is it?"

"It's just…how can I say this?"

"Say what?"

She lifted the book up. "It's just, I read something in this book—it's a Christmas novel actually—that made me think about something I've been thinking about ever since Smiley arrived. A subject I've been trying to avoid, if I'm being honest."

What on earth was she talking about? "What is it? Or should I ask, what's in the book?"

"I'm almost at the end, and the little boy gets a puppy for Christmas. Of course, in the book it's a really happy scene. But it started me thinking about another little boy, or maybe a little girl. I don't know which. The thing is, from the first few hours Smiley's been here, every time I've seen him since, and even the last forty-five minutes or so since you been gone…everything about him confirms what I've been thinking about, but don't want to say."

"Which is what?" John found himself tensing up.

"Which is…I'm not buying Alfred's explanation of how Smiley got lost and ended up in the woods, and how he wound up being here with us. I don't believe he got dumped off by some negligent owner trying to get rid of him. This is a truly excellent dog. Socially, he's very well-adjusted. Doesn't show a single telltale sign of negligence or abuse. And he's so well-trained."

"So, what are you saying?"

"I'm saying…what if Smiley belongs to a family who loves him? What if their car broke down on that road a few miles from here and somehow he got out and ran off into the woods? He's got that strong prey drive. Maybe he was chasing something, I don't know. But I just can't buy the idea that somebody dumped a dog like this in the woods on purpose. And if he does belong to a loving family, what if they had a little boy or little girl who are now missing him something awful? And who are about to have one of the worst Christmases of their childhood because they lost the dog they love in the woods, and they don't even know if he's okay, or if he's alive or dead?"

Her words felt like a punch in the stomach. "But how can we know? If what you're saying did happen, which we don't know it did, how could we ever find this family? He didn't even have an ID tag on his collar."

Jenny looked at him, almost answered, then hesitated.

"What?" John said. "Tell me."

"I hate to say this, John, because this dog has been doing wonders for you since he arrived. But when I was working in that shelter, I learned about these chips they have now. Put them in dogs all the time. Just under the skin. And if you bring a dog to a vet or one of these shelters that have a scanner, they can scan that chip, which links to a computer file, and have the owner's contact information in minutes. I'm thinking, the right thing to do is…use that cab ride tomorrow to drive Smiley down to a shelter—they have one in Summerville about fifteen minutes from here, and let them run that scan. If he doesn't have a chip, you're in the clear. But if he does…."

John didn't even want to think about it.

31

John had tossed and turned all night, wrestling over what Jenny had said yesterday when he came to pick up Smiley. Try as he might, he could not dismiss her logic. It didn't make any sense that someone would dump a dog as good-looking, good-natured and well-trained as Smiley off in the woods, as Alfred had suggested "to get rid of him."

And finding out about that chip technology had also destroyed the other argument John had placed his confidence in. That since Smiley had no ID tag on his collar, even if he hadn't been dumped in the woods there was still no way to locate his former owner. But there was. Or at least, there might be.

Throughout the night, John also kept reliving fond memories of Astro, his childhood dog. He couldn't imagine how horrible it would have been to lose Astro a week or two before Christmas. How could John continue to enjoy having Smiley around if it meant he was ruining a little boy's Christmas? Or a little girl, or a family, or...whoever?

It just wasn't right.

He looked at his watch. It was 9:15am. The cab would be arriving in less than fifteen minutes. He had been avoiding Alfred all morning. He'd decided not to tell him of his plans until after they had returned from the shelter. If they got to keep Smiley, no harm done. But if he had to turn him in…well, he'd rather inform Alfred of the news after the fact. If Alfred heard about the idea beforehand, he'd apply all kinds of pressure for John to keep him no matter what.

He grabbed Smiley's rope-leash and stood up. He'd better head over to Jenny's tent. Yesterday she said she'd go with them to the shelter. He hadn't even informed her of his decision yet and hoped she could still make the trip on short notice. "C'mon, boy. Let's go for a little walk."

Riley wanted to wag his tail after hearing John say they were going for a walk. He loved taking walks. It didn't matter where. But John was so sad, it was hard to find joy in anything right now. He wished he understood why. All he knew was that John's sadness began yesterday evening after they had left that nice lady's place. Riley had done everything he could to comfort John, but nothing seemed to help.

They walked along a hardened dirt path. Seemed like they were following the same trail they had walked on yesterday. Everything smelled exactly the same. After a few minutes, they turned a corner and he saw the woman's tent up ahead. It was such a colorful and cheerful place, compared to almost everywhere else around here. And she was such a nice lady. So kind.

"Hey Jenny," John called out.

She was hanging a towel on a clothesline. She turned. "John? And who do you have with you?" She said in a high-pitched voice looking right at Riley.

"Actually, I'm here because of what you said yesterday. You know, about Smiley possibly belonging to a family, not being dumped in the woods? And about that chip thing. I decided you were right. We can't just keep him without finding out if there's a way to locate his old owner. That cab I called is gonna be here in a few minutes. I'm gonna have him take me to the shelter instead of Goodwill. I don't suppose there's a chance you could still go with me. I've never been to one of these places before."

"Oh, John. I'm so sorry. I hope you're not mad at me for bringing it up. I just felt like I had to say something."

"I'm not mad. I'm hoping you're wrong about this. But I can't live with myself if we don't at least check and make sure."

"I'm glad," she said. "Not that you're having to do this, but that you care more about doing the right thing. Of course, I'll go with you. I'll just lay these last few towels over the chairs, so they can start to dry. I can hang them on the line later. Let me just go in the tent and get my purse. You want to leave now, right?"

"We've got a couple of minutes but, yeah, we should start walking down to the road."

She ducked inside the tent and came right back out. They

took a few steps down the main path when Jenny stopped. "I just had an idea." She reached into her purse.

"What?"

She pulled out her cell phone and looked around a few moments. "There. That's a good spot."

"What are you talking about? A good spot for what?"

She gently grabbed hold of John's wrist and walked him back toward her little palm tree decorated with Christmas ornaments. "Well, I thought we should take a picture of you and Smiley together before we leave. Just in case we get there and they do find a chip. Wouldn't you want a nice picture to remember him by?"

"I guess. Yeah, that would be nice. But I don't wanna be in it. Let's just take one with Smiley."

"Okay, that's fine. Why don't you bring him to the palm tree and see if you can get him to sit beside it. It'll be real cute, with him on one side and my little kissing snowman couple on the other. Will he stay there without you?"

"He will for this." John pulled out a piece of hotdog from a baggy in his coat pocket.

That instantly got Riley's attention. He loved hot dogs. He also understood the word *sit*. He started paying close attention to John to see what he wanted so he could get the treat. John took his leash and brought him over to a little tree. He asked him to sit, which Riley did instantly. He waited for the treat but then heard the command, "Stay." Okay, he could do that.

John backed up a few steps and held the hotdog out in front of him. He let go of the leash and kept repeating the stay command. Riley didn't need to hear it twice; he wasn't going anywhere until he heard John say okay. He didn't want to do anything to risk losing that treat.

"Go ahead and take the pic," John said.

"Aww look, he's smiling." Jenny clicked the pic then looked at her phone. "Came out perfect."

32

Summerville Humane Society

Kim Harper walked Kenzie back to her kennel. She was such a wonderful dog. Really, all six of the dogs she had selected for Taylor Saunders' new project were great dogs.

Over a week ago, she had finished preparing the training protocols for the dogs and had met again with Taylor to review them. She loved how hands-on he was with every facet of this project. It said a lot about him, considering what a busy man he was. Anne thought Kim was delusional if she thought *that* was his only reason for being so "hands-on."

"He's here because he wants to see you." Anne had said. "I can't believe you can't see it." Kim was sure Anne had it wrong. Although it did make her wonder how she would feel if Anne had been right. Taylor was really nice and seriously handsome. Anne was right about that. But Kim hadn't picked up any telltale signs of romantic interest when they had been together.

As she walked back toward the lobby, she thought about

their last meeting. Taylor had brought along the newly-selected resident manager of Dignity Pond. Both men had listened intently to her presentation and said after that they'd loved it. Every day since, she had taken the dogs through the new routines to get them ready for the transition.

In about thirty minutes, that resident manager was supposed to show up so she could take him through the training routines. She was just about to reach for the lobby door when her phone rang. She looked at the screen. It was the front desk, the place she was about to enter. Instead of answering, she simply opened the door. "Hey Anne, I'm right here." She held up the phone.

Standing in front of Anne at the reception desk were a middle-aged couple holding a leash attached to an adorable black and white spotted dog. It looked like a spaniel mix of some kind. As she got closer, she noticed the man was holding a rope, not a leash. She wondered what that was about.

"Oh good, Kim, there you are. Sorry to bother you, but they're kinda slammed in receiving right now." She looked at the couple then back at Kim. "This is John and Jenny. I don't know their last names yet, but they are friends, not a couple, right?" Both of them smiled and nodded. "And this cute little guy here is a lost dog they found in the woods about a week ago, named…"

"We named him Smiley," John said. "Because of the way he seems to smile sometimes, but we're not sure of his real name. He wasn't wearing any ID tag."

"Okay," Kim said. "Where exactly did you find him? You

said in the woods. There's a state park not too far—"

"We were camping, in a manner of speaking," Jenny said. "But not at the state park. Is there somewhere we can talk with you in private?"

"Certainly," Kim said. "Follow me right down the hall. We have a little interview room where we can talk. Feel free to bring Smiley with you." She looked at Anne. "Thanks. We shouldn't be long. That resident manager from Dignity Pond should be here soon. If I'm not out here before he arrives, can you keep him busy and entertained a few minutes?"

"It would be my pleasure."

"Right this way." She led the couple with the dog into the interview room. The dog instantly found the bowl of water in the corner. After everyone sat, she said, "Okay, what would you guys like to tell me about the dog?"

They looked at each other, as if unsure who should speak first. Finally, John did. "The thing is, we live in a homeless camp about fifteen, twenty minutes away from here. It's actually in the woods, but set back quite a-ways from the road. You can't really see it unless you know about the little dirt path that leads back to it."

"Have you ever heard about it?" Jenny said. "It's been back there for several years now."

"I think I've heard about it," Kim said. "But I've never been there. Is that where you found the dog?"

John nodded. "About a week ago, he just came into our camp right by my tent. He didn't look like he does now. Remember that bout of rain we were having? Well, he was completely covered in mud."

"We thought he was a black dog at first," Jenny added. "He was clearly thirsty and starving. We have no idea how long he was lost in the woods."

"Anyway," John continued, "for some reason, he kind of picked me out and started following me around. We got him all cleaned up and fed, and he's been living with us ever since. I've kind of taken to the little guy and thought about keeping him, but we started to think maybe we should make sure he doesn't have an owner somewhere first. Since he didn't have any ID tag on his collar, I thought there's no way we could ever connect him with anyone, but Jenny here tells me you guys have this new chip technology, and that maybe we should bring him in here, see if he has one."

"I see," Kim said. "Well Jenny, you're right. In fact, every dog that gets adopted from here has one of those little chips inserted before they go. I can't say for sure whether this dog has one. But we can certainly scan him and see. If he does, we'll know right away. And then we can look up his information online. We'll know within a few minutes if he has a previous owner, and if they're wanting him back."

The woman seemed very responsive to this information, but Kim noticed that John looked very sad. She looked down at the dog, who was sitting closely beside him. John reached down and patted his head. The dog offered a comforting lick. "Do you guys want to wait here while I bring him back and get him scanned?"

"You can do it that quick?" John asked.

Kim nodded. "Won't take much time at all."

"Then I guess you better do it," John said. Then he looked away, like he was trying to suppress some emotions.

"Is he friendly?" Kim asked, though she already knew the answer.

"Smiley loves everybody," Jenny said.

Kim stood. John handed her the leash. "C'mon, Smiley. Let's go for a little walk." She looked at the couple. "We'll be right back."

Ten minutes later, Kim had the information she expected to find written down on a piece of paper. She thanked the technician for fitting this task into her schedule. "Can I use your computer a couple of minutes to check this number out?"

"By all means," the technician said.

Kim got up, walked over to the young woman's desk and sat in front of the keyboard. The dog they were calling Smiley followed her and sat right beside her. "Okay Smiley, let's see what we can find here. See who your real owners are and maybe find out your real name."

33

Savannah, Georgia

Jeffrey was sitting on the couch watching a Christmas DVD, one he watched every year. He didn't even laugh at the funny parts anymore. Dad was sitting at the dining room table doing the bills. Mom was in the kitchen fixing lunch. He didn't know where Lisa was. He heard a phone ring and quickly recognized it was his dad's. The ring was loud, somewhere in the living room. He looked over and saw the phone on the end table being charged.

"Dad, your phone," he yelled. "I'd get it, but I can't." He pointed to his hurt foot.

"All right." He got up and hurried across the room, picked it up and pulled the charger cord out. "Hello? This is Tom Mitchell. How can I help you?"

Jeffrey looked at him for a moment then switched back to the TV screen.

"What?" Dad said. "Yes, that's my full name and that is our

address." He listened a few moments more. "Yes, we did lose a dog. What? His name? It's Riley. What? My gosh, you're kidding! You're not kidding! You're serious?"

Jeffrey looked up, saw tears welling up in Dad's eyes.

"You found him? You found Riley?"

Jeffrey could not believe what he just heard. He dropped the remote and sat straight up. Now his eyes filled with tears.

"I can't believe it!" Dad said. "And he's okay? He's not hurt at all? Who found him? Where did you find him? Never mind, that's not important now." He looked at Jeffrey. "They found Riley, son. He's perfectly fine. They have him in a shelter in Summerville." He turned his attention back to the phone. "Yes, we definitely want him back. We lost him on the way home from a trip to Disney about a week ago, on Highway 301. He got out of the car and took off in the woods after some animal. We thought we'd never see him again."

Mom heard the commotion, and came out of the kitchen toward Dad. She saw the tears on his and Jeffrey's face.

"They found Riley, Mom," Jeffrey said.

She instantly began crying and reached for a box of tissues on the hutch, pulled out a few and ran over toward Dad. She handed him a couple, gave some to Jeffrey then sat beside him on the edge of the couch. "Thank you, Jesus," she kept saying over and over again.

"Can we come get him now?" Dad said. "We're in Savannah. Where in Summerville is this place?" He listened a few moments. "I'm sure we can find it with the GPS. Sounds like you're maybe four or five hours away, depending on

Jacksonville traffic. What time do you guys close?" He listened some more. "Yeah, I don't think we can get there by then. How about this? We'll get our things together and start driving down there. We can check into a hotel nearby for the night and be there to pick him up first thing in the morning. Will that work?"

He listened again. "Great, that will really help. I'll check my phone for your email in a few minutes. I can't thank you enough for this call. Seriously, you have literally saved our Christmas. Well, you and those wonderful folks who found him and brought him back. I don't suppose they can be there tomorrow, so we can thank them properly ourselves? Hmm, I understand. But please, please express our gratitude and let them know—" He started to choke up. "—there is nothing I could have bought, no amount of money I could've spent this Christmas, that would have meant more to my son, Jeffrey, than getting Riley back. Tell them, our whole family thanks them so much and wishes them a very Merry Christmas."

He hung up and set the phone on the end table. Mom ran over and hugged him. They both came over to Jeffrey, who by now had grabbed his crutches and made it to his feet. He wanted to hug both of them, but he was afraid he'd lose his crutches, so they hugged him.

Dad pulled back a little and said, "Guys, how about we go and get Riley back?"

34

When Kim walked back toward the lobby, after just locating and talking to Riley's actual owners, she was a little conflicted. Clearly, the family who had lost him was overjoyed by the news he'd been found. They instantly dropped whatever plans they had made the day before Christmas Eve, to drive all the way down here from Savannah. But now, Kim would have to deliver the sad news to the nice homeless man who had returned Riley, that he'd have to say goodbye to his newfound friend. It was obvious he had already bonded with the dog and wanted to keep him for good.

She looked down at Riley walking beside her. He was oblivious to all that was about to happen. As a dog behaviorist, Kim had learned a good deal about how dogs think and the best ways to communicate with them when training. But at moments like this, it was obvious significant communication gaps still existed between people and dogs.

Last week, when he got separated from the family he loved, he probably had no idea where they went or why they had driven off, leaving him all alone in the woods. Then after being on his own a few days, he stumbled into this camp of homeless people and was completely welcomed and embraced. Now that he was just beginning to form some new routines and bonds with these people, they were going to leave him all alone again at a strange shelter. Kim wished there was some way she could tell Riley why this was happening, and that it was actually a wonderful thing. She sighed, realizing there was no way she could minimize his confusion and pain.

She opened the lobby door and was surprised to see Taylor Saunders standing there at the reception desk talking to Anne. "Taylor? I didn't expect to see you today." He was alone. "Where's your resident manager? I'm sorry, I forgot his name."

"Hey Kim. Didn't think I was gonna get to see you today, either. His name is Todd, Todd Williams. He called me about a half hour ago saying a county inspector needed to see him over at the project right away before he would sign off on something. I remember you saying this was your last work day before the Christmas holiday, and I really didn't want to reschedule this until after Christmas, so I decided to come myself. Hope that's okay?"

"No, that's great." She was standing next to him now and reached out her hand. "I could certainly show you what I was going to show Todd. But at some point before you guys open, I'm still going to need to show him these things, too. I'm technically off between Christmas and New Year's, but I'd be happy to get with him on one of those days."

"So you're not leaving town for the holidays?"

"I'll be gone Christmas Eve through the day after Christmas to see my folks, but I'll be home the rest of the time."

"Good to know," he said.

She looked down at Riley. "I can get with you in just a few minutes. First I have to handle kind of a delicate situation in the interview room. Do you want to wait here or back in my office?

"I can just wait here."

"Okay, see you in a few."

John was starting to get nervous. The young lady who had taken Smiley off to be scanned had been gone longer than a few minutes. He looked at Jenny. "I wonder what the holdup is."

"I don't know. But I'm sure everything's fine."

Fine. How could it be fine? The only way it could be fine is if it turned out that Smiley didn't have one of those chips put in or, if he did, they found out who the owner was and he didn't want him back.

Suddenly, the door opened. The woman walked in with Smiley. He quickly hurried over to John and sat. He genuinely seemed relieved to be with John again. But John looked at the woman's face and could instantly tell she wasn't there to bring good news.

"How did it go?" Jenny said. "Did he have a chip? Could you read it?"

The woman sat across the table. "The answer is yes to both

questions. And I'm afraid I have some sad news for you guys. For you especially, John. I can see how fond you've become of the dog."

John sighed.

"We located the chip pretty easily. It's a painless thing for the dog. A few minutes later, I was able to look up his contact information online. Turns out, his owners are a young family who live in Savannah. They lost Riley—that's his real name by the way. You guys were real close calling him Smiley. They lost him driving home from a trip to Disney. They pulled the car over, I can't remember why just now, but Riley saw an animal nearby and broke away, chased him into the woods."

Jenny looked at John. "Told you, he had a strong prey drive."

"He definitely does," Kim said. "I talked with the father. His name is Tom. The family has been heartbroken ever since they lost the dog. I could hear Tom crying as I broke the good news that Riley had been found. He relayed the message to the family while we were on the phone, and I could hear them rejoicing in the background. He said they're going to get in the car right away and drive down here to get him. We'll be closed by then, so they'll stay in a hotel and come by first thing in the morning."

John sighed again, looked down at Smiley...*Riley*. This was a bittersweet pill to swallow, but deep inside he was genuinely glad they had done the right thing. "So that's it then." He looked at Jenny. She had just lifted some tissues from a Kleenex box on the table and was dabbing her eyes.

"I'm real happy for them, for this family," she said. "But it's kind of sad for us. Especially John. He and the dog had already become such good friends."

"There's something else I need to tell you," Kim said. "The last thing the father said to me on the phone." She looked right at John and said, "He said to tell you how thankful they were for you bringing Riley back and that you had literally saved Christmas for their family this year. Then he said there was no present he could ever buy, no matter how expensive, that his young son would want more than getting Riley back."

Tears welled up in John's eyes. Hearing that certainly helped. He reached for a tissue. "Do you know the boy's name? The son?" John said.

"His name's Jeffrey," Kim said. "I wrote it down."

"I'm so sorry, John," Jenny said.

"It's okay. I'll be okay." He wiped his eyes. "We're doing the right thing for the dog, and for his family. That's what matters, especially now at Christmastime." He looked at Kim. "Can I have a minute alone with him, just to say goodbye?"

"Of course you can," she said and stood.

John saw her reaching for a tissue. She and Jenny quietly left the room.

Riley didn't understand anything that was happening. Everyone was so sad, especially John. And now the others had left the room. One other thing confused him...a minute ago, he thought he'd heard the woman they just met say the word *Jeffrey*.

John got out of his chair and squatted down on the floor, just in front of Riley. He cupped Riley's face in his hands. Tears were coming down his cheeks. Riley wanted so much to get closer to him, to try and comfort him, but he could tell John wanted him to stay put.

John began to speak.

"I've been calling you Smiley for about a week now. Mainly because, of that look you get on your face. But the truth is, having you around has made me smile for the first time in a long time. I know you don't know a word I'm saying, but I still need to say it. Thank you for picking me out to be your friend. For showing up at our camp last week and spending all this time with me. I was hoping we could be friends for a whole lot longer. But that's not how it's supposed to be. Instead, I have to say goodbye."

More tears came. He didn't want to interrupt them to grab a tissue. He needed to get this over with.

"I'm pretty sure you're going to be sad when I leave you here, but you're only going to be sad for a very short while. Tomorrow will be the happiest day you've had in a long time, maybe in your whole life. You know why? Because *Jeffrey* will be here."

Jeffrey? Did he just say Jeffrey?

"That's right, boy. You know that name, don't you? Jeffrey. That's who's coming tomorrow. And he's gonna bring you home."

Home? Jeffrey? Riley looked around the room. What did this mean? Was Jeffrey coming now? Was Jeffrey here?

"I'm sure this is confusing you a little bit. But you won't be confused for very long." He stood up. "Let's bring you out to that nice lady. She's going to take care of you until Jeffrey comes tomorrow."

John opened the door and walked out. Riley followed, walking right beside him.

35

A few minutes ago, while John was in the interview room saying goodbye to Riley, Kim had gotten an idea. As soon as it formed in her head, she knew she had to pursue it. Right away. But she also had to be careful. She said a quick and quiet prayer that if God had put this idea in her head, he would give her the right words to say.

"Taylor, could I have a word with you in private? I just thought of something I need to ask you about. It doesn't have anything to do with the reason you came here today to see me, but I'm going on a hunch that it might even be more important than that." She looked at Anne then at Jenny. "I'm sorry, would you excuse us for a few minutes?"

"Sure," they both said.

"Taylor, we can talk in the hallway on the other side of that lobby door."

"Okay, you lead the way."

Once they were inside the hallway and the door had closed, Kim said, "I'm sorry for this oddball way of handling this, but

I can't think of a better way at the moment."

"That's okay, Kim. What's up? What are you thinking about?"

"I'm going to talk fast, because the person I'm wanting to talk to you about is in the interview room right now, and he'll be coming out any minute. That woman standing out there beside Anne's desk, her name is Jenny. The man inside the interview room is named John. They are both homeless."

"Really? Wow, that's kind of a coincidence."

"I know, isn't it? But maybe it's not. They came here about a half hour ago with a dog they had found in the woods about a week ago. The dog walked into their camp, a homeless camp about twenty minutes from here. At first, they thought maybe it was just an abandoned dog and, besides that, it didn't have an ID tag. But then the way the dog acted made them think it was too good-natured and well-trained not to be somebody's pet. Jenny knew about the chips we put in dogs, so she persuaded John to bring him in. That's why they came. But I'm telling you, Taylor, it was totally obvious to me that this dog has had a profound effect on John. He turned it in because it was the right thing to do, but he's heartbroken over it. He's in there saying goodbye right now."

"I see where you're going here. You're thinking he might be a good candidate for Dignity Pond."

"Do you still have any openings?"

"We do. Five or six. But you remember the reason why our place isn't completely packed already, right? Considering there are hundreds of homeless just like John and Jenny in this county."

"I do. You said most of them don't want to live in an organized place with a bunch of rules they have to follow."

"More than that, the overwhelming majority have substance abuse issues that they're not ready to part with. That's proved to be an even bigger obstacle for us."

"I understand that," she said. "And I even agree, totally. I can say John seemed to me to be completely sober. His speech wasn't even slightly slurred, and his eyes looked totally clear and white. I know that's not enough to say yes, but is it enough maybe for you to talk to him? See if he's even interested or willing to apply? I could be totally off base here, and if it doesn't work out I won't be upset with you at all. Like I said, I'm going on a hunch."

Taylor thought a moment, then smiled. "Sure. I'd be happy to talk to him. After all the years dealing with my dad, I'm a pretty good judge of these things. I should be able to spot if he's not being totally straight with me. But do me a favor...when you introduce us, don't tell him who I am."

"Okay. I'll just say you're one of the main guys at Dignity Pond."

"That'll work."

"And how about this," Kim said, "you guys can meet in the interview room, and if you reach a point where you're feeling good about him, good enough to invite him to apply, could you text me while you're still in the room? You could just text the word, *Yes*."

"Sure, I can do that."

36

John tried to compose himself as he walked down the short hallway connecting the interview room with the lobby. He saw Jenny there standing by the receptionist's desk. That young woman who had been helping them was there, next to a taller, nicely dressed young man who appeared to be in his early thirties.

John walked right up to the young woman and handed her Riley's leash. He saw her name tag. That's right, Kim. "Well, we've said our goodbyes. At least, I have. I know Riley doesn't completely get what's going on. But I know how happy he'll be tomorrow."

"That's great, John," Kim said. "I know how difficult this must be, but you really are doing the right thing. I know you know that, but I want you to know how much I respect you for following through with this." She handed off Riley's leash to the receptionist. "Anne, can you walk Riley back to my office? I'll be back there in a few minutes, but there's something else I have to do first. Give him some treats and make sure he has some water."

"Sure, I'd be happy to." She got up and started walking, "C'mon, Riley."

John decided it would be easier for him not to watch Riley walk away. He was just about to say goodbye, when Kim spoke up.

"John, before you go, there's someone I'd like you to meet. This is Taylor. He's one of the main guys at a new project called Dignity Pond. Have you ever heard of it?"

John nodded. "I have."

"I've heard of it too," Jenny said. "It's that new project for the homeless being built about thirty minutes from here. Read something about it in the newspaper a while ago. Supposed to be almost finished by now, isn't it?"

"We're doing the final inspections now," Taylor said. "Hope to open our doors right after the New Year's holiday."

"It's just a coincidence," Kim said, "that you guys are here at the same time as Taylor. He was actually coming here to meet with me about a special project we're working on together. But John, I asked him if he could meet with you for a few minutes, and he said he would. Are you okay with that?"

"With me and Jenny?" John asked.

"Just with you for right now," Taylor said. "But I'd be happy to talk with Jenny also after we're done."

"Sure," John said. "Can't see any harm in hearing what you have to say."

"We won't be long," Taylor said to Jenny.

They headed down the hall. John opened the interview

room door. They both walked in and sat down.

"John, so we don't keep your friend out there waiting too long by herself, I'll get right to the point, if that's okay with you."

"I'd prefer that."

"Kim said you guys are part of a homeless camp situated in the woods not too far from here. How long have you been homeless?"

"Going on twenty years, I'd say."

"That's a good long while. Obviously, it's become more of a lifestyle for you then. What I mean is, some people are just homeless for a few months because of some financial setback that just happened. But if you're doing it that long, you're probably doing it because you prefer living that way. Would that be a fair thing to say?"

John found the question oddly disturbing. If he had asked John that a year ago, even six months ago, John would have definitely said yes.

"You're hesitating. Have you ever thought about making a change?"

John thought about how deathly afraid he was of lightening, of how tired he was sleeping in a leaky tent, of always going to the bathroom outside, of going to bed cold and waking up freezing, and the fear of being violently attacked by a stranger on any given night. "To be honest with you, I might be."

"Really? What kinds of things have you heard about our little project?"

"Not a whole lot. I'm guessing it's supposed to be something of a halfway house for homeless people wanting to find their way back into the mainstream. And that you all have built all these nice little places for people to live in, but I don't really know all that much more about it. I know it's probably something I could never afford."

"Why do you say that?"

"Well, it's not as though I have a steady job, and I definitely don't have any money sitting around in a pension fund. I'm making it okay, living at the camp. Expenses are pretty low out there."

"What if I told you that your lack of money is not a problem? That we'd be willing to work with you, regardless of the size of your income? Would that make this idea any more appealing?"

"It…definitely might. Are you saying…something like that is possible?"

"I am. Now here's the stickier thing. I'm sorry, but I have to ask this. How are you doing with the drinking? Are you taking any illegal drugs?"

John was relieved to hear him say this. The way he'd started this question made John tense up. "I never had a problem with drugs, but I used to really be a heavy drinker. For a long time. It's fair to say, that's how I became homeless in the first place. But it's also fair to say, it's totally in my past. I haven't had a drink for at least a decade. Doctor told me if I didn't quit, I'd be dead. And I believed him."

Taylor smiled. "What about your friend out there, Jenny?

Do you know where she's at on that subject? Think she might consider a place like Dignity Pond?"

"She doesn't drink as much as she used to. I've never seen her take drugs. Not sure where she's at in terms of quitting. You'll have to ask her." He thought of Alfred. He didn't have to wonder about how Alfred would answer that question.

"You guys take a cab to get here?"

John nodded.

"What would you think of this? I've got about a thirty minute meeting with Miss Harper out there. Kim. How about after that I take you and Jenny over for a tour at Dignity Pond, then I'll drive you back to your camp myself. Would you be open to that?"

John couldn't believe what this young man was saying? "Yes, I think I would."

"Great." The young man pulled out his cell phone. "I just need to send someone a very short text."

37

Kim's cell phone chimed. She picked it up and read the text from Taylor.

Yes.

"Okay, Kenzie. That's our queue." Kim had already taken the yellow lab puppy out of her kennel but had kept her in the hallway outside the lobby area, anticipating Taylor's text. Riley was safely tucked away back in her office with Anne. Kim looked through the little window in the door just in time to see Taylor and John coming back out to the reception desk. She wasn't sure how much Taylor could tell her about what had transpired between him and John, but one thing was clear: John's countenance had dramatically improved.

She was pretty sure things for him were about to get even better.

Opening the lobby door, she looked down at Kenzie. Kenzie's eyes had already zeroed in on the cluster of people up ahead. Instantly her face brightened and her tail began to wag. Kenzie loved people. She was the perfect ambassador for this new program.

Taylor noticed Kim first, then saw Kenzie. He instantly squatted down and held out his arms. "Kenzie, there you are. Come and see me." She ran right up in between Taylor's arms. He hugged her and she began loving on him. "What a good girl, you are." He stood and backed up to allow John and Jenny a clear view of the dog. "John, I forgot to mention something to you in our little chat. The reason I'm here meeting with Kim is, she's training a team of companion dogs to live at Dignity Pond. Part of the responsibility of our residents will be to care for these dogs and, really, just to spend some time together and enjoy each other's company. Kenzie here is one of the dogs who will be living with us very soon."

Kim looked at John's face. He was smiling even more than before. "Kenzie, greet."

Kenzie instantly walked up to John and sat politely at his feet. John bent down to pet her and she quickly snuggled up between his legs. "What a beautiful dog you are." He looked up at Kim. "How old is she?"

"She just turned eight months this week."

"She's still just a pup," he said. "I can't believe how calm she is for being so young."

"She has one of the sweetest dispositions for a dog I've ever seen." She looked up at Taylor. "This is going to be a hard one to let go of."

"Well, you can come by and see her anytime." Just then, his phone rang. He looked at the screen. "I'm sorry, I have to take this." He walked to the other side of the lobby and talked for a few moments.

She saw him nod a few times, then a serious look came over his face. He nodded one more time and hung up. He came back and said to John, "I'm really sorry. Something came up that I have to tend to right now, so a few of the people who work for me can take tomorrow off. I'm not going to be able to take you guys on a tour of our little village right now. I can still drop you off where you live, though."

"That's fine," John said.

"But hey, I am off tomorrow," Taylor said. "I could swing by around midmorning and take you on a tour then. Jenny, you are welcome to join us."

"Well, that would be great," John said. "But tomorrow's Christmas Eve."

"I'm okay with it as long as you are."

"Sure," John said.

Jenny nodded her head. "I don't know what you're talking about, but I'd like to see it, whatever it is."

Taylor looked at Kim. "So sorry, Kim. Looks like I can't meet with you right now, either."

"Well, I'm off tomorrow…technically. But if you'd like, since you're meeting them midmorning, my parents only live two hours away. I wasn't planning to be at their place until 4:30. How about you text me the time you'll be arriving at Dignity Pond with John and Jenny, and I'll meet you there with Kenzie. We can do our little demonstration there just as well as here."

"Really? You'd do that?" he said.

"Of course, it wouldn't be like work. It'd be fun."

"Great. I love that idea. John and Jenny, are you guys able to head out with me now?"

"Yes, we definitely can."

"Let's go then, Nice to see you again, Anne. Hope you have a great Christmas. Kim and Kenzie, I will see you both tomorrow."

After the three of them had left, Anne looked at Kim and smiled a mischievous smile.

"What?" Kim said. "What's that face for?"

"Oh, nothing. It's just what Mr. Right said there at the end, and the way he was looking at you when he said it. *I love that idea.*"

38

The following morning, Jeffrey hurried as fast as he could on his crutches out to the car. Dad was putting the last of their overnight baggage in the back of the SUV. Before getting in, Jeffrey turned around to find Mom standing in the doorway of the hotel room. Lisa was still inside. "Mom, we have to hurry. The shelter opens in fifteen minutes."

"We'll be fine, Jeffrey. Lisa just forgot her sweater. This isn't like a doctor appointment. We can be a few minutes late."

The lady from the shelter had called Dad yesterday in the late afternoon when they were still on the road coming down. She said she had to be somewhere by 10am and wanted to know if they were picking up Riley before then. If so, she'd like to be there. Dad said they'd like to come as soon as the shelter opened. The lady said then to come at 9am.

Jeffrey was so excited. He couldn't wait to see Riley again.

After his dad had gotten out of the shower that morning, he'd announced to the family, "It's Christmas Eve everybody. Can you believe it?"

Jeffrey knew it was, which meant tomorrow was Christmas Day. Normally his two favorite days of the year. But up until yesterday, and for over a week, he had been dreading both days because Riley was gone. He didn't know how he could ever enjoy Christmas again. Now, this was turning out to be the best Christmas ever. He didn't even care about any of the other presents back home under the tree. The thing he wanted most was at a Humane Society fifteen minutes down the road.

Finally, Mom, Dad and Lisa got in the car. In a town this size, there was no such thing as a rush hour. They made it to the shelter right on time. Dad pulled into a parking place close to the front door. As they got out, Mom gently warned Jeffrey to be careful on his crutches. She always got nervous when he hurried. Dad held the door open. Jeffrey strained his eyes through the glass for any signs of Riley, but he didn't see him.

"Jeffrey," Mom said. She was holding up something she had pulled from her purse. "Don't want to forget this."

It was Squirrel. "So glad you remembered," he said. "Can you hold it for now till we get inside?"

"Sure."

They walked across the lobby. "Hi, we're the Mitchells from Savannah," Dad said to the receptionist. "I'm Tom. We have an appointment with Kim Harper. We're here to pick up our lost dog, Riley. We got a phone call that someone dropped him off here yesterday."

The receptionist looked down at a notebook. "Yep, I see a little note here about that. I'm just a volunteer. The normal receptionist is off for the holiday. I thought Kim was off, too.

But apparently she is here. Let me call her office." She picked up the receiver. Just then, a door opened. "Oh, there she is."

Riley awoke that morning fairly confused. At first, he didn't know where he was. Then he remembered being put in this small room yesterday with a lot of other dogs, each in their own pen. The lady who had put him there was very nice and knew his real name.

She had come back a little while ago and took him for a walk, so he could go to the bathroom. When they came back inside, she didn't put him back in the pen. Instead, she walked him through the kennel area into a big hallway. Then she had asked him to sit, which he did.

She talked to him for a few moments with the most pleasant face and in the nicest tone. He only understood two words of what she'd said, but they were his favorite two words in the world, and she had said both of them twice.

Jeffrey and *home*.

She opened a door leading to a much bigger room. Riley saw something that, for a second, he almost didn't believe. It looked like Jeffrey was standing there, with the rest of the family.

Then he spoke, and Riley knew it was real.

"Riley!"

It was slightly against protocol, but Kim didn't care. She released Riley's leash and let him run to Jeffrey, who had now let go of his crutches and was sitting on the floor. As soon as she let go, Riley made the most unusual squealing-howling-bark she had ever heard. It startled her. He continued making this strange sound until he was fully immersed in Jeffrey's arms.

Jeffrey was sobbing with joy. She realized this strange noise must have been Riley's way of expressing the same emotion. A few seconds later, the volume subsided but he continued to cry and whimper as he licked Jeffrey nonstop. His tail wagged frantically back and forth. Jeffrey handed a stuffed squirrel to him, which brought out another happy reaction from Riley. Kim's only regret was forgetting to film this moment. It would have certainly gone viral by the end of the day.

Now the rest of the family had gathered close to Riley and Jeffrey, tears in everyone's eyes. Riley stopped briefly to greet each one, the squirrel sticking out of his mouth. He was clearly happy to see them all, but in between greeting each one he reconnected with Jeffrey. Kim knew what this was.

To Riley, Jeffrey was everything. He was probably the first human Riley had fully connected with, had loved completely, and the one he would love just as intensely for the entirety of his life, even if they had remained apart. The separation from Jeffrey, for Riley, had probably been the most traumatic experience of his life. And now, his suffering was over. He was in the arms again of the little boy he loved most.

And for Jeffrey? Watching this, Kim didn't doubt for a moment what his father had said on the phone yesterday... *There is nothing I could have bought, no amount of money I could've spent this Christmas, that would have meant more to my son, Jeffrey, than getting Riley back.*

Jeffrey's father, pulled away from the others long enough to greet her and extend his hand. "Hi, I'm Tom Mitchell. We spoke on the phone yesterday. I don't know how I can begin to thank you for this."

"Happy to play a small part in this moment, Mr. Mitchell. It's times like these that make me forget the more challenging parts of my job. Merry Christmas to you, and to your family."

39

This was without a doubt the nicest car John had ever ridden in. A shiny black Jaguar with a soft tan leather interior. The dashboard looked more like the cockpit of a modern fighter jet. John was no longer living under the illusion that this kind young man who had picked them up this morning was one of the managers for this homeless village they were about to see.

Yesterday when Taylor had brought them back to the camp, Hampton had been coming out of the woods near the road and saw them. At first, John thought the look of shock on his face was simply the surprise at seeing him and Jenny getting out of such a nice car. That was certainly part of it. But after Taylor had left, Hampton told them who he was.

What he'd actually said was: "*What in the world are you guys doing getting out of Taylor Saunders' car? Don't you know who he is? He's a billionaire several times over.*"

John had heard the man's name before but knew very little about him. Hampton filled the two of them in on everything he knew. They told him about his invitation to tour Dignity

Pond with them today. Hampton seemed to know a lot about that, too. He said several of the folks who lived at the camp were scheduled to move there right after the New Year when it opened. He'd also added the reason why most weren't considering it was they absolutely forbid the use of drugs or alcohol on the premises.

That news set Jenny back. Not the part about the drugs but the drinking. "I'm trying to cut back," she'd confided in John when they had walked back to their tents, "but I don't think I could just cut things off like that, cold turkey." She'd said John should take the tour by himself and asked him to thank Taylor for the invitation.

John had done that about twenty minutes ago, when he'd first gotten in the car. Taylor looked sad but said he'd understood. He'd asked John to relay a message to Jenny for him, and to any of his other friends there who might be interested. He did say that alcohol wasn't allowed at Dignity Pond, but that they also had a great rehab program and they'd be willing to help her break completely free of her dependence, if she was open to let them try. If it didn't work out, she could leave at any time.

"Here's the turnoff just up ahead on the right," Taylor said, pointing. "I'm so glad you were willing to come, John. And I've got to say, I was really impressed by your sense of integrity, returning that dog to the shelter yesterday even though you clearly had already become good friends. Kim told me about the reunion scene she witnessed when the Mitchells came to pick Riley up. Sounded like quite a moment."

"Thanks, but to be honest, when I got to the shelter at first, I was secretly hoping they wouldn't find a chip or, if they did, the owners wouldn't want him back. But as I thought about that reunion scene you just mentioned and Riley's reaction to being back with the little boy who'd lost him, it killed any doubts I had about it being a mistake to return him."

John hadn't let on that he knew Taylor's real identity yet. He must have his reasons for wanting to keep that concealed. Billionaire or not, John found it very easy to be with him. He seemed as normal a person as any John had met.

Taylor made the turn into the facility. The entrance looked as nice as any fancy subdivision John had ever seen. They drove down a fairly long fully-landscaped driveway that led to a main building with a circular driveway in front. In the center, was a trio of tall queen palms. On the right was a paved parking area. Down both sides of the road on the left were little cottages, spaced evenly apart, not much bigger than a large shed. But each had a little covered porch in front and all were bigger than any of the tents John had seen in any of the homeless camps he'd ever been in.

"This is the community house," Taylor said. "Kind of like a clubhouse if you've ever been in a modern subdivision." He pulled around the circular driveway and parked near the front doors. There were only two other cars in the parking lot. Taylor had said earlier, the place would be mostly empty because it was Christmas Eve.

They got out of the car and Taylor opened the glass door, held it for John. "You guys don't lock the place when you're not here?"

"We do, but we have a 24/7 security guard who lives here. I told him when we were coming and asked him to leave the door unlocked." They walked into a big open room with lots of upholstered sofas and armchairs. To the left were two pool tables. On the right was a reception desk and a small office. Beyond the sofas and chairs were rows of round tables surrounded by folding chairs.

"The front part is kind of a hangout area, the back half is the dining room. There's a big kitchen through that doorway on the right. That door on the left leads to a small gym area and the restrooms, which have showers. Each of the units has their own bathrooms also."

"Very nice," John said. That really did describe what he saw. It wasn't high-end like some fancy hotel lobby, but it was very clean and, of course, everything looked brand-new.

Taylor led him through the rest of the building then out the back door, which had a big covered screened-porch with lots of wooden rockers and, best of all, a view of what you'd either call a small lake or a big pond.

"What do you think?"

"It's beautiful. I love it." Even as John said these words, they sounded strange to him. He realized he hadn't used words like this in a conversation in a very long time.

"The road you saw on the left with the little cottages on either side becomes a shady nature trail that goes all the way around the pond and comes back around to the parking lot on the right. Let's follow this walkway back around to the front and I'll open up one of the cottages for you. We don't really need to see them all. Other than a few little things here and there, they're pretty much the same."

"I haven't seen any dog kennel," John said, "or did I miss it? Didn't you say that there were going to be companion dogs here?"

"Oh, there are definitely going to be dogs here. Six of them at first, but possibly twelve by mid-January, if things go according to plan. But this idea came about fairly recently. I was thinking we would need to build a dog kennel, but Kim had a different idea, which she thought would work better. We did build a small clinic and grooming building for them. But I'll show you what she has in mind in just a minute. It's sort of a surprise."

A surprise? John wondered what he meant. When they came to the street where the little cottages were located, John noticed Kim Harper sitting on a rocker on the small porch of the very first one with a light-colored dog that looked like Kenzie.

Kim was really enjoying this. Yesterday afternoon, after Taylor had dropped John and Jenny off at their camp, he had called to say he really got a good feeling about John. They would still have to do the paperwork, but he couldn't imagine John not being approved to be a resident of Dignity Pond. So he'd asked her to help him with a little surprise.

She had seen them pull up and go inside the Community house. Now they were coming here from around back. She stood up to greet them. "Hey John, glad you could make it. Good morning, Taylor. And I guess since it's Christmas Eve, I should add, Merry Christmas!"

"Good morning," John replied. He came up the steps far enough to pat Kenzie on the head.

"Merry Christmas to you, too," Taylor said. "Is everything all set?"

"All set," she said. "You two can go on in."

"You first," Taylor said to John. "Go on in, the door is unlocked."

John walked inside. Taylor and Kim followed. John's eyes roamed all around the interior. It wasn't spacious, but Kim thought it was very cute, like something out of those tiny house shows. Taylor had really gone out of his way to make these places feel special.

"There's your kitchenette area along the back wall," Taylor said. That little room to the right is your bathroom. It's pretty snug, but there's a toilet, sink and standup shower. On the right here is your bed and on the left a nice recliner, small table and TV set. Which works by the way. Just basic cable, but it works."

"You keep saying *your*," John said.

Taylor put his hand on John's shoulder. "That's no accident, John. It's yours if you want it to be. I have no doubt you'll be approved if you decide to apply."

John knelt down and began rubbing behind Kenzie's ear. She had come over and sat beside him. Had he decided? He'd been living outside for so long. But as he looked at all that was being offered, he realized…he was ready. John hugged Kenzie for a moment and didn't immediately reply to what Taylor said. When John looked up, tears welled up in his eyes. "I would definitely like to be here, if you'll have me. I can't even believe this is happening."

Taylor extended his hand. "It is happening, John. Merry Christmas. By the way, I don't know if you noticed the crate at the foot of your bed. Kenzie's part of the deal. She won't be yours exactly, but Kim thought we should have the dogs actually living with some of the residents in their cottages. You would be one of the dog handlers at Dignity Pond, if you don't mind a few extra responsibilities."

John looked down at Kenzie. She was looking up into his eyes. "I wouldn't consider that work. It would be a privilege."

After a few moments, Taylor asked if he could speak with Kim out on the porch, to let John have a few minutes alone with Kenzie in the cottage.

Once outside, Taylor stood in front of Kim. "Thanks so much for setting this up. It couldn't have gone any better. I especially want to thank you for setting up this whole dog program. It's going to make a wonderful difference, and I can't wait to see all the positive things that come from it down the road."

"You're very welcome," Kim said. "I love doing things like this."

His expression changed completely. He seemed to be trying

to think of what to say next. "Kim, I also wanted to thank you for coming out here on your day off. I know you're getting ready to spend Christmas with your family, but I wanted to ask you something. And please, don't feel any pressure to say yes. And if you need to take a little time to think about it, that's okay too."

What in the world was he getting at? "What is it, Taylor?"

"Would you be open to the idea of me seeing you? I mean, outside of this little project we're working on together."

"You mean...like a date?"

"Yeah, that's exactly what I mean. I'm sorry if this is putting you on the spot, but—"

"It's not, Taylor. Not at all. The answer is yes. I'd love to go out with you sometime."

"Really?"

"Yes, really. When are you thinking?"

"How about New Year's Eve? Have any plans?"

"No. What do you have in mind?"

"I haven't thought it all through yet. I wasn't sure you would say yes. But did you know, I have a plane?"

Kim laughed. "Yes, I think I knew that."

40

Savannah, Georgia

When Jeffrey woke up, the second thought he had was that today was Christmas Day. The first thought was: *I can't believe Riley is sleeping on my bed.*

Of course, Riley instantly woke up seconds after he did. He leapt from the bottom of the bed to the spot right next to Jeffrey and smothered him with licks and dog hugs.

Jeffrey must have been exhausted last night because he was the last one to get up and head downstairs. Usually on Christmas morning, it was Jeffrey's job to wake up the whole house.

He put on his robe and made his way to the stairs. He could already see the Christmas lights from the tree glittering against the stairwell wall and hear the Christmas CD playing. Dad always played the same one every year. He had to go down slowly, but Riley ran on ahead.

When he reached the bottom of the stairway, the living

225

room looked like a magical place. It had been fully decorated for several days but it was as if today was the first day Jeffrey had ever seen it. Mom was arranging presents under the tree in piles. Lisa was sitting on the edge of the sofa drinking hot chocolate. Dad had just gotten up to let Riley out back to go to the bathroom.

Jeffrey came and sat on the other end of the sofa, set his crutches on the floor. Mom came over and gave him a big hug, "Merry Christmas."

"Merry Christmas."

Dad walked in. "Look who finally woke up?"

"I know, right?" Jeffrey said.

"Can we open presents now that he's finally here," Lisa said.

"Sure," Dad said. "It was so good seeing Riley running around the backyard. Now I feel like I can really enjoy this day. How about we do something before we dive in and open our presents?" He suggested they say a little prayer thanking God for bringing Riley back home safe and sound. Everyone agreed. He led a prayer of thanks and they all said Amen.

For the next twenty minutes, they took turns each opening one present from their pile. Mom and Dad's piles were always a little smaller. When there were only two left in Jeffrey's and Lisa's, Jeffrey heard Riley by the back door barking to be let in.

"Lisa," Mom said, "can you do it?"

She did and instantly Riley came running in and began rummaging around the tree, moving in and out of the opened packages, smelling everything. It was the same thing he did every Christmas morning.

Mom got up and left the room.

"Poor Riley," Lisa said. "Look at him. He's looking for his present. What are we going to do?"

"Can't we give him something?" Dad asked. "Maybe some dog treats? Lisa, why don't you take some of this wrapping paper into the kitchen and just toss some dog treats in a baggy and wrap them up real quick."

Just then, Mom came back into the living room, holding a long wrapped present. "Riley?" she said. He looked up and ran over to her. "What is this? What do I have?"

She put it under his nose. He started jumping up and down. She tossed it under the Christmas tree. He ran after it, grabbed it, dragged it out to the front and began tearing into it.

"Look at him," Dad said, standing up. "He knows it's for him."

"What is it, boy?" Jeffrey said. "Is it your Christmas present?"

Bits of wrapping paper were flying all over. Now you could see what was inside. A huge rawhide bone. When Riley had almost all the paper off, he grabbed it in his mouth and ran over to Jeffrey. He jumped up on the sofa between him and Lisa and started gnawing on the end.

"Mom," Jeffrey said, "When did you get this? We didn't get home until late last night."

Mom walked over and put her arm around Dad's waist. "I didn't get it last night."

"Then when?"

"Remember last week when you were so sad, and I suggested we shouldn't give up hope? We prayed and asked God for a miracle?"

Jeffrey nodded.

"I bought it that afternoon, as a statement of faith. To be honest, two days ago, I was actually thinking about bringing it back to the store for a refund. But I decided to trust God and wait a few more days."

"And look what He did?" Dad said.

Jeffrey reached over and patted Riley on the head. He had that look on his face he gets when he's totally relaxed and happy. The man who found him in the woods was right. He does kinda look like he's smiling.

Author's Note

Finding Riley is actually the 2nd book in the *Forever Home Series*. If you've read it first, no harm done. Dan wrote it so that it could easily be read as a stand-alone book. But we think you'd really enjoy reading the first book, *Rescuing Finley*. You'll recognize many of the same characters and even some of the same places.

Here's a link for *Rescuing Finley* on Amazon. You can download it now and start reading it within minutes. It is available in print on Amazon and will also likely be available at B&N and WalMart.
amzn.to/1Hn0vrg

Dan has already begun working on Book 3 in this series. It will be called *Saving Parker* and should release in 2017.

If he is a new author to you and you haven't yet read any of his other novels you'll be happy to learn that, besides this one, there are 16 others in print. Most are in a similar genre and style, although in 2014 Dan also began to write the *Jack Turner Suspense* series.

His suspense novels have been so well received, Dan has decided to write both kinds of books from now on. As of this writing, his novels have received over 4,500 Amazon reviews while maintaining an average of 4.6 Stars.

Finally, a brief note about the homeless village of *Dignity Pond* (featured in this book). *Dignity Pond* is a fictitious place, but villages for the homeless similar to it have begun to appear all over the US. Dan would encourage his readers to Google: "village for homeless." You'll quickly learn all about this innovative and compassionate approach to help the tens of thousands of homeless people living in unsafe and sometimes dangerous conditions throughout the country.

Want to Help the Author?

If you enjoyed reading *Finding Riley*, the best thing you can do to help Dan is very simple—*tell others about it*. Word-of-mouth is the most powerful marketing tool there is. Better than expensive TV commercials or full-page ads in magazines.

Dan would greatly appreciate it if you gave a rating for the book and left a brief review. Even a sentence or two will help.

Below is the Amazon link for *Finding Riley*. Scroll down a little to the area that says "**Customer Reviews**." Right beside the graphic that shows the number of stars is a box that says: "**Write a Customer Review**."

http://amzn.to/2c7xdWY

Sign up to Receive Dan's Newsletter

If you'd like to get an email alert whenever Dan has a new book coming out or when a special deal is being offered on any of Dan's books, click on his website link below and sign up for his newsletter (it's right below the Welcome paragraph).

From his homepage, you can also contact Dan or follow him on Facebook, Twitter or Goodreads.

www.danwalshbooks.com

Want to Read More of Dan's Novels?

You can check out all of Dan's novels by going to the Books page of his website, or his Author Page on Amazon. Here's the link:

http://amzn.to/2cG5I90

If you'd like to write Dan, feel free to email him at dwalsh@danwalshbooks.com. He loves to get reader emails and reads all of them himself.

Acknowledgments

There are a few people I absolutely must thank for helping to get *Finding Riley* into print. Starting with my wife, Cindi. Not just for her encouragement and support. Over the years, Cindi has become a first-rate editor. She's provided vital editorial help not just with the storyline and characters in this book, but all my novels. I want to also thank my great team of proofreaders, who caught many of the things Cindi and I missed. Thank you Terry Giordano, Jann W. Martin, Patricia Keough-Wilson, Debbie Mahle and Rachel Savage.

Dan Walsh

About The Author

Dan Walsh was born in Philadelphia in 1957. His family moved down to Daytona Beach, Florida in 1965, when his father began to work with GE on the Apollo space program. That's where Dan grew up.

He married Cindi, the love of his life in 1976. They have two grown children and three grandchildren. Dan served as a pastor for 25 years, then began writing fiction full-time in 2010. His bestselling novels have won numerous awards, including 3 ACFW Carol Awards (he was a finalist 6 times) and 3 Selah Awards. Three of Dan's novels were finalists for RT Reviews' Inspirational Book of the Year.